Princess DisGrace

Also by Lou Kuenzler

Princess DisGrace First Term at Tall Towers

SHRINKING VIOLET
SHRINKING VIOLET DEFINITELY NEEDS A DOG
SHRINKING VIOLET IS TOTALLY FAMOUS
SHRINKING VIOLET ABSOLUTELY LOVES ANCIENT EGYPT

Princess DisGrace

Second Term at Tall Towers

Lou Kuenzler
Illustrated by Kimberley Scott

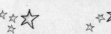

Scholastic Children's Books
An imprint of Scholastic Ltd
Euston House, 24 Eversholt Street
London, NW1 1DB, UK
Registered office: Westfield Road, Southam, Warwickshire, CV47 0RA
SCHOLASTIC and associated logos are trademarks and/or registered
trademarks of Scholastic Inc.

First published in the UK by Scholastic Ltd, 2014

ISBN 978 1407 13629 5

A CIP catalogue record for this book
is available from the British Library.

Printed and bound by CPI Group (UK) Ltd, Croydon, CR0 4YY

Papers used by Scholastic Children's Books are made
from wood grown in sustainable forests.

1 3 5 7 9 10 8 6 4 2

www.scholastic.co.uk

To my girls again
-LK

CHAPTER ONE
Keeping Lookout

Princess Grace was perched high in a tree on top of a cliff on the shores of Coronet Island. She was staring up at the cloudless blue sky through a pair of old binoculars, which were slung around her neck on a piece of string.

"Are you all right down there, Billy?" she asked, lowering the binoculars and calling to the scruffy black and white unicorn below. She'd tied Billy to the trunk of the tree with her Tall Towers Princess Academy school uniform sash.

Grace was pretty sure this was not what the Tall Towers rules meant when they said: *A princess must **always** make sure to use her sash when wearing her school tunic.* The strict First Year form teacher, Fairy Godmother Flint, would not be at all pleased if she knew that Grace was using the satin sash as a unicorn rope – especially as it was starting to look a bit frayed where Billy was chewing the end of it.

But it was Friday, when the princesses were allowed to ride their unicorns for an hour after school. As soon as class was over, Grace had grabbed her binoculars and dashed to the stables. She hadn't stopped to find a proper rope . . . or even a saddle. She'd left Billy in his halter and ridden him bareback along the beach at full tilt.

Ambling back to school along the high cliff path, she'd spotted a perfect lookout tree.

Hundreds of birds were swooping about the cliffs, searching for the best place to make their spring nests.

But it wasn't birds that Grace was interested in.

"Who's up there? What are you doing?" said a sharp voice from beneath the tree.

Grace looked down through the branches and saw the school gamekeeper with a crossbow slung across his back. His tiny niece, Hetty, stood just behind him.

"Oh. It's you, Princess Grace," the keeper sighed. "I should have guessed." Keeper Falcon was a fierce-looking man with narrow eyes and quick movements like a fox. He always seemed to find Grace in the wrong place at the wrong time.

"Hello, up there," waved the little girl. Young Hetty could not have been more different from her uncle. She had a round, open face, with big, wide eyes and a sprinkle of freckles on the end of her nose.

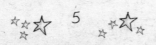

"I love your unicorn. Can I stroke him?" she asked.

"Of course," said Grace. "His name's Billy. Give him a really good scratch behind the ears. He loves that."

But Keeper Falcon coughed and nudged his niece fiercely. "Where are your manners, Hetty?" he growled.

"Sorry." Hetty blushed and dropped to one knee in a deep curtsy. "Good afternoon, Your Majesty. I hope you are having a pleasant day."

"Very pleasant," smiled Grace. "But you don't need to curtsy to me." It seemed ridiculous. The little girl was a year or so older than Grace's own sister, Princess Pip. Just like Pip, she clearly wished she had a unicorn of her own.

I know just how that feels, thought Grace. Until she had come to Tall Towers last term, having her own unicorn was all she had ever dreamed of too.

"Go ahead," she smiled. "Stroke Billy as much as you like."

"That's very kind of you. But Hetty must know her place," said the gamekeeper with a stiff bow. "She is lucky enough to live with me now her poor mother is dead. Your kind headmistress, Lady Du Lac, is generous enough to let her stay here on Coronet Island. It's Hetty's job to help me with the chores. . ."

"Like feeding the peacocks and doves," said Hetty brightly.

"But you must remember that you are a servant, Hetty. Not a royal princess like the other girls," the keeper barked.

At the harsh tone of his voice, Hetty jumped backwards as if she had been slapped.

"Sorry, Uncle," she murmured. "I just wanted to stroke the unicorn, that's all."

"Well, mind your manners," snapped the

keeper. Grace was shocked at how strict he was. He bowed again as he turned back towards her. "Are you birdwatching up there, Young Majesty?"

"No. It's not birds I'm looking out for," said Grace, dropping down to a lower branch. "It's dragons."

"Dragons?" Keeper Falcon's head shot up and he peered at Grace through narrowed eyes. "Have you seen any?"

"Not yet," said Grace.

Hetty burst out laughing.

"There aren't any dragons on Coronet Island," she chuckled. "They'd eat up all the princesses if there were. Princesses are a dragon's favourite food, everyone knows that."

"Shh! That's no way to talk to a princess." Keeper Falcon hushed his niece. "But Hetty is right," he continued. "There haven't been any dragons on this island for fifteen years. I saw to that myself."

"The Dragon Purge – they were all driven away from here," said Grace sadly. She did not want to be eaten by a dragon, of course. But she was fascinated by the magnificent fire-breathing creatures all the same. She'd read in the school library how the fierce Coronet Crimson dragons who used to visit the island every spring had been moved to new nesting sites to keep the Tall Towers princesses safe. Now the rare red dragons were believed to be extinct.

"But you never know what I might see . . . I'll keep a lookout just in case," she said brightly.

"Do as you please. But you won't see anything," said Keeper Falcon with a shrug. "I've staked my job on keeping dragons away from this island. Now that the Coronet Crimson is extinct, this place is safe for ever." He clicked his fingers for Hetty to follow him. "Come on. We have plenty of real work to keep us busy. Let's leave this young princess to her pleasant games."

Grace blushed. Was she really being silly to hope that she might see a dragon?

But Hetty hung back for a moment as her uncle strode away.

"Let me know if you spot anything," she whispered, standing on tiptoes and staring up at the tree. "Especially if it's the size of a flying rhinoceros with bright red scales. . ."

"I will," promised Grace, as Hetty blew Billy a kiss and hurried away.

CHAPTER TWO
The Dragon

Grace watched as Hetty ran to catch up with her uncle.

"If only Princess Grace would behave like the other pupils at this school," she heard the gamekeeper tut as Hetty ran alongside him.

"I think she seems fun," said Hetty. "And her unicorn is the cutest one I've ever seen."

Grace smiled. It was true. She couldn't imagine anyone else in her class climbing to the top of a tree to keep a lookout for dragons. Her long brown plaits were bristling with twigs and leaves, and her school tunic was tucked into a big pair of blue-and-yellow-striped bloomers. (They should have been regulation white if Grace was obeying the school rules.)

Grace wriggled round in the tree, turning the binoculars towards the twisting turrets and sparkling spires of Tall Towers Princess Academy, which shimmered like a crown at the edge of the harbour. At least Hetty didn't think she was a *total* disaster as a princess, but Grace could see why Keeper Falcon wasn't quite so sure. Sometimes, she still couldn't believe she was a proper princess pupil at such a beautiful, elegant fairy tale school.

Grace remembered how strange everything had seemed when she'd first arrived from Cragland, the small, rocky kingdom where she and her little sister, Princess Pip, lived with their father, his herds of hairy yaks and his fierce warriors. But now, halfway through her second term, Grace felt part of Tall Towers at last. She felt she belonged here – even if she *was* the clumsiest princess in the whole class. It didn't seem to matter that her curtsy was a little wobbly or that she still couldn't balance a book on her head in deportment class. At least she was better at unicorn-riding than anyone else and she adored Billy and spent every free moment galloping about the island with him. It didn't even matter that her spiteful cousin, Princess Precious, was a First Year too, and was always trying to turn the class against her. No matter what went wrong, Grace knew she always had her two best friends, Princess Scarlet and Princess Izumi, to help her out.

Peering through the binoculars, she could just make out the faraway figures of the two princesses standing under an apple tree on the smooth, green lawn at the front of the school. Elegant Scarlet was practising some sort of dance move, her long red hair fanning out behind her. And Izumi had her neat, dark head bent over a pile of cards.

"Those must be the invitations for the Ballet of the Flowers," groaned Grace, swinging her legs over a branch and beginning to climb down towards Billy. "I'd better get back and see if I can help write out the envelopes . . . just as long as I don't make too many blotches."

The First Years had been asked to stage a spring ballet for all the school governors. Rehearsals were due to begin first thing on Monday morning. The other princesses in the class were buzzing with excitement, but Grace wasn't quite so sure. She didn't really see herself as a dainty, dancing flower – more of a tangly beanstalk with big feet.

"I wish it was a riding show, don't you, Billy?" asked Grace. "I never feel clumsy when I'm on your back." But just as she spoke her foot slipped. A branch cracked.

"Arghhhhh!" Grace came tumbling down, the leaves of the tree whooshing past her as she fell. She landed with a soft thud on the moss below. Billy shook his head, almost as if he was laughing at her.

"Very funny!" said Grace. She sat up and was tickling him on the nose, when suddenly she blinked and grabbed the binoculars.

Staring into the sky above, she saw a bright flash of red as something shot over the top of the trees. "A dragon," she gasped, her heart thumping like a drum. The huge creature was fast, and it was flying low.

"Wow!" Grace could clearly see its scaly, red belly, its thick, leathery tail and silver-tipped wings. "A Coronet Crimson. . ." But it couldn't be. Keeper Falcon had driven all the Coronet Crimson dragons from the island fifteen years ago. He had told her so himself. And now they were extinct.

17

Grace's hands were shaking so hard that the binoculars slipped from her fingers. She fumbled to pick them up.

"I didn't dream it, did I?" she whispered. Perhaps she had banged her head when she fell from the tree.

But Billy had seen something too. He pulled hard against the blue sash that kept him tied to the tree. He stamped his hooves, his nostrils flaring wide with fear and his ears lying flat against his head.

"Steady," soothed Grace as she scrambled to her feet and peered through the binoculars again.

"There it is!" She caught a last glimpse of the dragon as it shot away like a firecracker, heading in the direction of school. If Grace closed her eyes she could still picture its huge clawed feet almost brushing the top of the tree above her, and its bright crimson

scales shining like rubies in the sun.

"Keeper Falcon, come back," she called, grabbing Billy and running desperately along the path in the direction where he and Hetty had gone. But it was hopeless. The keeper might be anywhere in the woods by now.

"Quick," she said, turning Billy around and throwing the sash over his neck to make a pair of reins. "We need to ride to Tall Towers and warn everyone that there's a dangerous dragon on the island."

She leaped on to Billy's bare back and galloped flat out towards the school.

CHAPTER THREE
Keep Off the Grass

Grace clung to Billy's neck as they charged towards Tall Towers.

Skidding through the golden gates at the end of the driveway, Grace just had time to read the big brass sign that said, "STRICTLY NO UNICORNS IN THE GARDENS. KEEP OFF THE GRASS", before Billy careered across the middle of the lawn.

Never mind about rules, thought Grace. *This is an emergency.* She needed to warn her friends about the dragon – it might have come to the island to look for princesses to eat. She glanced up at the cloudless spring sky. There was still no sign of the creature anywhere, just three puffs of white smoke.

"Scarlet! Izumi!" she called. Her friends spun around in surprise.

Billy's head was down, and clods of turf flew up from the perfect, green lawn as he thundered, flat out, across the grass towards them.

"Steady," said Grace. She was galloping even faster than the time she had ridden a knight's charger in a real joust last term.

"Look out," shouted Princess Izumi, as Billy headed straight for the apple tree where they were standing.

"I saw a dra—" cried Grace, then suddenly realized she was out of control. Without a proper bridle she had no chance of steering

Billy. Spooked by the big dragon flying over him and excited by the wild gallop back to school, he was like a cork exploding from a bottle of fizzy lemonade. Nothing was going to stop him now.

"Careful," screamed Princess Scarlet, leaping out of the way.

Billy swerved.

"Whoa!" Grace shot forward over the top of his head.

As she spun through the air, she glimpsed a flutter of white, like snow. But it couldn't be snow. It was a beautiful spring day. Perhaps it was blossom falling from the tree. But the flakes were too big.

Thud!

Grace landed on her bottom. As she bounced across the ground, she realized that the white filling the sky was the squares of card.

"The invitations for the ballet show," she gasped, toppling over as she bounced, and skidded to a halt with her nose flat on the grass. "Oh, no."

Artistic Princess Izumi had spent hours drawing pretty spring flowers round the edge of each invitation. And Scarlet, who had the neatest handwriting in the class, had been up until midnight writing them out.

Now one hundred white invitations were

scattered in the mud churned up by Billy's hooves.

The charging unicorn had come to a stop by a tinkling fountain a little way off. A corner of white card was poking out of his mouth like a half-eaten slice of toast.

"Spit that out!" cried Grace. But Billy chewed . . . and swallowed. He took a long drink from the fountain. Three more invitations were skewered on the end of his horn like white marshmallows on a stick.

"Oh my goodness," gasped Scarlet.

"What a mess," shuddered Izumi.

"I'm so sorry," said Grace, looking up at her friends' shocked faces. "I didn't mean to make you drop the invitations. But I came to warn you. There's a dragon on the island."

"There can't be," said Izumi, glancing up at the sky.

"There haven't been dragons here for years. Have there?" said Scarlet, her hands shaking.

"I was up a tree. Then I banged my head," said Grace. "But I definitely saw it. It was huge and bright red." Still sitting on the grass, she stretched out her arms to try to show how large the dragon had been. "I think it was a female. She had silver wings."

Before Grace could say anything else, there was a creak of hinges and Fairy Godmother Flint, the strict First Year form teacher, poked her thin nose out of the staffroom window in the high tower behind them.

"Thank goodness you're there, Fairy Godmother. We need to get everyone inside. I've just seen a dragon," Grace called up, leaping to her feet.

"I find that most unlikely," said old Flintheart, barely even glancing at the sky. "Before we let our imaginations run away with us, let us remember – dragon or no dragon – it is strictly against the school rules to ride across the grass." The stern teacher did not need to raise her voice or shout – even from so high up, every word was icy-clear and furious. "You are in disgrace *yet again*, Young Majesty," she sighed.

"But, Fairy Godmother," said Grace, looking at the deep gashes Billy's hooves had made in the perfect green lawn. "I *really* did see a dragon. It was as big as a flying rhinoceros, and had crimson scales and silver-tipped wings."

Grace stood on tiptoes, scanning the pointed towers and high rooftops of the school, almost hoping to see the dragon perched like a giant red cat on the tiles. At least then everyone would believe her.

"First things first: I suggest you clear up this mess." Fairy Godmother Flint pointed down to the scattered cards. "I will see you in the courtyard in five minutes to explain yourself."

Before Grace could say another word, Fairy Godmother Flint closed the window firmly.

"That is *so* unfair. Why won't she believe me?" Grace spun around to face her friends. But she saw that they weren't looking up at the teacher, or searching the sky for the dragon. They were staring at the ground, looking at the tattered invitations spread across the lawn.

"All our hard work for nothing," said Izumi.

"None of them can be saved," agreed Scarlet.

"It's not as bad as that. Look." Grace picked up the nearest card and tried to wipe it on her sleeve.

The First Year Princesses
at Tall Towers Academy
Invite you to celebrate spring.
Please join us for
The Ballet of the Flowers.

But it was no good. The date and place where the show was to be held were smeared with mud. Scarlet and Izumi were right: the whole pile of invitations was ruined. It was all Grace's fault.

CHAPTER FOUR
Cousin Precious

Grace grabbed hold of Billy as Scarlet and Izumi gathered the muddy cards from the ground.

"I'm such a clumsy idiot," she said. "It was silly of me to charge around like that. I just wanted to warn you about the dragon."

"What dragon?" said a voice from across the lawn. "I bet you made the whole thing up just to get yourself out of trouble with Flintheart."

Grace looked round to see her mean cousin,

Princess Precious, hurrying towards them with a spiteful little grin on her face. The giggling twins, Princesses Trinket and Truffle, were trotting along behind her as usual.

"You're just trying to get yourself out of trouble," they echoed, squealing with laughter like two posh pink piglets.

"Great! That's all I need," groaned Grace under her breath.

"Grace's middle name should be *Trouble*," crowed Precious. "Before she came to Tall Towers, she practically ran wild at home. Her father might be a king, but he dresses from head to foot in yak fur, for goodness' sake."

"Don't you dare bring my home into this," snapped Grace. "I *did* see a dragon. It was a Coronet Crimson. I don't care what you say." She pointed up to the sky. "Look, you can still see three puffs of smoke, if you don't believe me."

Izumi raised her hand, squinting towards the sun. "I think those are just clouds, aren't they?" she said.

It was true. The puffs of smoke did look harmless enough.

"Exactly!" said Precious. "It doesn't prove a thing. If this dragon is as big as you say, everyone on the island would have seen it."

"Perhaps it was just a trick of the light in the sky," said Scarlet kindly. "I see shadows and things that make me jump all the time."

"It wasn't a shadow. It was a dragon," said Grace. But it was obvious that even her two best friends didn't believe her.

"You poor, poor things," said Precious, dashing forward and throwing her arms around Scarlet and Izumi as if they were *her* best friends. She usually only bothered with the richest princesses at Tall Towers. In general, she completely ignored Izumi,

whose kingdom was not much bigger than the one Grace came from. And she rarely paid any attention to shy, quiet Princess Scarlet. But now she hugged them tightly and the twins joined in.

"I thought Grace and that horrible, scruffy unicorn were going to trample you to the ground," gasped Precious. "It must have been dreadful for you. I saw the whole thing."

Scarlet did look very pale and shaken. Her green eyes were still wide and bright with shock.

"We're fine," sighed Izumi. "I just wish I could say the same for the invitations."

"I'll help you make some new ones; I promise," said Grace, ignoring Precious and the twins.

"Don't worry," Izumi shook her head.

"We'll manage fine by ourselves . . . honestly," said Scarlet.

"Oh. . ." Grace felt a stab of unhappiness: she knew at once why her friends wouldn't let her help. She wasn't artistic like Izumi. Her handwriting wasn't neat and beautiful like Scarlet's. Grace couldn't even draw a good stick princess. Her school work was so messy, it always looked as if a spider – or even a whole troupe of spiders – had danced across the page with inky boots on.

"Imagine what invitations made by Grace would look like," snorted Precious. "We could hardly give those to the school governors."

"She has the worst handwriting ever," roared the twins.

"I won't bother, then," said Grace. Hurt was burning inside her like a fire. She scuffed the toes of her shoes into the ground, desperate not to cry. Not in front of Precious. She swung her foot and kicked a stone across the lawn, aiming at the apple tree. But it bounced sharply off the trunk.

Ping!

It hit Scarlet hard on the leg.

"Ouch!" The red-haired princess winced with pain and looked up in shock.

"I'm so sorry," cried Grace. She rushed towards her friend, dragging Billy behind her. "Are you all right, Scarlet? I didn't mean to hit you. . ."

"That must have really stung," gasped Izumi.

"Poor Scarlet, you'll have a terrible bruise," said Precious.

"Terrible," agreed the twins.

Grace hugged Scarlet and Billy tried to nuzzle in too.

"I was aiming for the tree," Grace explained.

"I'm fine," said Scarlet but she moved away

rubbing her leg. "You ought to go and see Fairy Godmother Flint before you get in any more trouble."

"Yes, hurry along Princess *Dis*-Grace," sneered Precious.

"Oh, be quiet," snapped Grace. She felt terrible about hurting Scarlet – the last thing she needed was Precious stirring up trouble and making things worse.

But as she glanced towards her friends, she saw that Izumi was shaking her head.

"Precious does have a point this time, Grace," she said.

"If you hadn't been galloping so fast, the invitations would never have been spoiled," added Scarlet quietly.

"It's just typical of Grace!" said Precious.

"Typical!" echoed the twins.

Grace opened her mouth to explain about the dragon one last time . . . but there was no point. Precious had her arms around Scarlet and Izumi again. They were all staring back at Grace, shaking their heads.

"I don't see why everyone's making such a fuss, anyway," Grace growled. "The invitations were only for a stupid flower ballet. I don't even want to dance in it."

"Don't be silly," said Izumi.

"Of course you want to dance in it. It's going to be the highlight of the whole term," said Scarlet.

But Grace turned and stomped away.

If Scarlet and Izumi would rather be friends with Precious, she'd leave them to it.

"Wait!" called Scarlet.

"Come back!" said Izumi.

But Grace kept on walking. Her hands were shaking as she led Billy into the courtyard and came face to face with Fairy Godmother Flint.

CHAPTER FIVE
One Hundred Lines

Old Flintheart sighed as she led Grace up to the staffroom and signed a black-edged punishment slip with her crow-feather quill.

"It is Saturday tomorrow," she said, handing the notice to Grace. "But you will spend it in the library writing lines."

"What about the dragon?" said Grace. It would serve Flintheart right if the great beast suddenly swooped into the courtyard, roaring and blowing fire. But almost as soon as she thought it, Grace shuddered. She knew

Hetty was right. A dragon's favourite food is always a nice fresh princess. Someone sweet and dainty like Scarlet would make a perfect mid-morning snack.

"I have sent a message to Keeper Falcon telling him what you *claim* to have seen," said Flintheart. "But I hardly think we need to call a troupe of royal guards. You have let your imagination run away with you, Young Majesty. There have been no dragons on this island for many years." She placed her quill in the ink pot as if the matter was closed.

"You *have* to believe me," cried Grace desperately. "I did see a dragon. It flew right above my head. It's tail was three times as long as this sash."

Grace waved the thick satin ribbon in the air. Then she remembered that Billy had chewed the ends and tried to hide it behind her back.

"I could saddle up my unicorn – properly this time – and help search the island," said Grace quickly. She was desperate to protect her friends, but didn't think about the danger to herself. Ever since she had won a jousting tournament at the end of last term, she felt more like a knight than a princess anyway.

"You will do no such thing," said Flintheart. "In fact, you are banned from riding for the whole weekend."

"But. . ." Grace bit her lip. She knew there was no point in arguing. And when Keeper Falcon came striding into the staffroom, he laughed as if the whole thing was just a joke.

"I was up on those cliffs myself. I saw nothing," he said. "The whole idea is ridiculous. Coronet Crimson dragons are extinct. They have been for fifteen years."

"Ever since you drove them away from this island," muttered Grace under her breath.

"There is no way you can have seen the creature you describe," said Keeper Falcon, impatiently pacing the room and looking out of the tower window as if there was somewhere he'd rather be.

"But couldn't she have been sleeping or hibernating for somewhere all this time?" asked Grace. "Dragons do live for hundreds of years."

"I don't think you need to tell Keeper Falcon about dragons, Young Majesty," said Flintheart crossly. "He is a world expert on the subject."

Keeper Falcon was already hurrying towards the door. "I suggest you spend less time looking for dragons and climbing trees from now on, Young Majesty," he said sharply, "and spend more time thinking about how to be a proper Tall Towers princess."

"Quite," said Flintheart, wagging a bony finger at Grace. "You have the Ballet of the Flowers to think about, for a start."

*

The next morning Grace was in the library even before it was time for her punishment to start.

"Ancient Dragons of the World," she muttered, pulling a big red leather book from the shelf.

And there it was. The very last picture in the book.

Coronet Crimson (Female)

Following the dragon purges on Coronet Island, these magnificent but dangerous creatures were driven from their spring nesting grounds.

Coronet Crimson (Female). Her dragon – just like the one she had seen – right down to the huge, silver-tipped wings and gold-clawed feet.

The Coronet Crimson Dragon is now thoroughly extinct, she read. Grace ran her finger across the page tracing the shape of the dragon's wings. It was so sad to think that these magnificent creatures had died out.

"But I know I saw one. Either everyone else is wrong, or I am," murmured Grace, feeling as if the whole world was against her.

She flicked back through the book, looking at pictures of spotty green dragon eggs and mothers with their wings tucked around tiny pups. There was a section on dragon myths and legends from different countries. Grace even saw a picture of a whole village, all dancing together in a long line, with a red silk dragon costume lifted over their heads and their legs becoming the limbs of the beast.

"Time to get started now," said Fairy Godmother Webster, the old librarian who was supposed to be watching Grace while she wrote her lines. Grace closed the book, her head full of swirling dragons. She unrolled her scroll, dipped her frayed quill in a pot of ink and began to write.

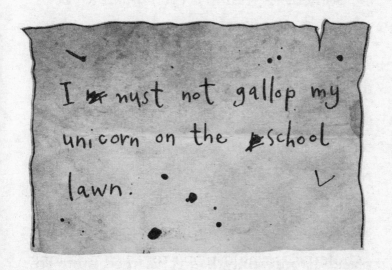

I must not gallop my
unicorn on the school
lawn.

Grace wrote until her wrist hurt. The trouble was, Flintheart had said they had to be one hundred *perfect* lines: "*No blotches or blots or you'll have to start over again.*"

Grace was so miserable that she smeared and smudged her work even more than usual. She started again five times.

"Dragon poo!" she muttered under her breath, even though she knew it was not a very princessey thing to say.

"Sometimes I don't even *want* to be a proper princess," she grumbled, as a blot of ink spread across the page. No wonder her friends hadn't let her help them make new invitations. Her stomach twisted into a tight knot as she remembered how she had ruined the beautiful cards.

How could she have been so stupid as to gallop across the lawn like that in the first place? If only Billy hadn't charged quite so fast. It was her own fault – she should have put a proper bridle on him. She couldn't be angry with Billy.

But she *could* be angry with Precious. Her spiteful cousin had gone out of her way to stir up trouble with her friends. Now the two girls were barely talking to Grace. The three of them had been planning a lovely picnic all week. But they'd probably gone off with Precious now instead.

"Oh, dragon poo!" said Grace again. She stabbed her quill into the page so that a new blot of ink spread across the parchment.

"I'm going to be here all day," she groaned.

But just at that moment, Izumi poked her head around the library door.

"Psst," she whispered. "Is it safe to come in?"

Grace glanced over at Fairy Godmother Webster. The old librarian had fallen asleep hours ago with her head resting on the copy of *Ancient Dragons of the World* that Grace had taken from the shelf. She was snoring happily as if she had dozed off on a soft feather pillow.

"All clear." Grace smiled. She wanted to clap her hands when she saw that Scarlet was there too.

"We thought you might need some help," whispered Izumi as she crept into the library.

"We know old Flintheart always wants lines to be perfect," said Scarlet, never taking her huge, worried eyes off the sleeping librarian.

Grace let out a long sigh of relief. She should have known her friends wouldn't stay angry at her for long. "I do need a *bit* of help," she laughed, pointing at the inky scribble on the page.

"Oh, Grace," smiled Scarlet.

"That's *terrible!*" chuckled Izumi. "Even worse than we thought it would be. It's a good job we brought this."

The smile faded from Grace's face as her friends began to unroll a clean white scroll.

"I know you should do the punishment yourself," said Scarlet.

"But we felt so sorry for you," continued Izumi. "So we've written the lines for you instead."

"You felt sorry for me?" said Grace, a hot blush creeping up her neck. They were starting to sound like Precious.

"We did half each," said Scarlet excitedly, pointing to row after row of clear, curly lines on the bright, white page. "We made our handwriting look as much like yours as we could."

"Only much neater, of course" said Izumi.

"And with a few small blotches, just to make it look real."

Grace looked down at all the hard work her friends had done. Her hands were shaking as she picked up the scroll.

"Hand these in now and we can go for our picnic," said Izumi.

"Just the three of us," said Scarlet.

But Grace didn't move.

"Let's put this mess in the bin." Izumi grabbed a corner of Grace's own ink-spattered scroll. "Oh dear, these lines would never have got past Flintheart," she laughed. "They really are a disgrace. . ."

"Don't touch that," said Grace, snatching her scroll away. "That's all you two think I am, isn't it? A total disgrace."

"No!" Izumi stepped back in surprise. "We don't think *you're* a disgrace . . . just these scratchy old lines. We knew you'd make a mess of them so. . ."

"Yes! Just like I make a mess of everything, according to you," snapped Grace.

She barked so loudly that Fairy Godmother Webster sat bolt upright and blinked.

"What's all this noise?" said the old librarian opening one eye. "Have you finished your punishment, Princess Grace?"

"We just came to see how she was getting on," said Izumi quickly.

Grace glanced down at the perfect lines her friends had written for her. She knew that if she handed them in she could escape from the library right away and head off on a picnic just like they had all planned. Maybe she could even take the binoculars and search for the dragon.

But she just couldn't do it. She picked up the perfect scroll, scrunched it into a ball and tossed it in the bin.

Scarlet gasped.

"I haven't finished yet. I'm sorry, Fairy Godmother," said Grace. "Those lines were no good."

"Well, you better hurry up," said the librarian, laying her head back down on the desk.

"What did you do that for?" hissed Izumi. "Our writing was perfect."

"Just like you two," said Grace, furious tears pricking the corner of her eyes. "Perfect Princess Scarlet and perfect Princess Izumi always rushing to the rescue of poor disastrous Princess Disgrace!"

"It's not like that," said Scarlet. "We were only trying to help."

"I don't want your help," snapped Grace. "And I don't want to be your friend, either." The words were out of her mouth before she could stop herself.

"Fine!" said Izumi.

"If that's what you want," said Scarlet. The pity in her eyes was far worse than the anger in Izumi's. The two girls turned and walked out of the library.

Grace picked up her quill with shaking fingers. "*I must not gallop my unicorn*," she wrote.

But now it was the tears streaming down her face that blotted the page.

CHAPTER SIX
Monday Morning Ballet Class

By Monday morning, Grace was in a thoroughly bad mood. She had barely spoken a word to Scarlet and Izumi and there was still no sign of the dragon.

Grace knew she really had seen the enormous creature, but decided that the dragon must have been flying over the island and not stopping.

If Coronet Crimsons really are extinct, thought Grace, *then the one I saw must be the last one left in the whole world. She won't be coming here to nest. She'll be roaming the seas, desperately hoping to find a mate.* Grace felt sad for the lonely dragon, far out there across the ocean somewhere. There would never be any proof that she had been here at all. Everyone would go on believing that Grace had made it up or imagined her.

Now, on top of everything else, it was double ballet for the first two lessons. It wasn't that Grace didn't *like* ballet – she was usually happy to give it her best shot. It was just that the other twelve princesses in her class were so much better than she was. They'd all been taking dancing lessons ever since they could walk.

"That's what proper princesses do," as Precious said at least five times a day.

The first thing Grace had learned when she could walk was how to milk a yak. Cragland was not like the kingdoms the other princesses came from. It was cold and rocky and far away from anywhere else: the only thing that ever danced in Cragland was the wind in the trees. Grace's mother had died shortly after her little sister, Princess Pip, was born. Now there was no queen to organize balls or ballet shows. The king and his band of hairy warriors would rather roast yak meat and gather round the fire to tell tales of ferocious beasts than dress up and attend a dance.

"Grace doesn't even have a ballroom, for goodness sake," Precious had told the entire class. "Let alone a ballet studio. . ."

So, while everyone else was already advanced, Grace was just a beginner when it came to dance. A very clumsy beginner. Madame Lightfeather, the ballet teacher, always had to stop the lesson and ask the rest of the girls to wait, balancing on their pointed toes, while she showed Grace how to lift her heels and reminded her *yet again* not to stamp her feet.

Up in the little attic dormitory she shared with Scarlet and Izumi, Grace frowned as she tried to tie her messy hair into a neat ballet bun. Her friends usually did this for her, but today Grace refused to ask for help.

"They're always interfering and doing things for me," she mumbled. "No wonder I don't get any better by myself."

By the time she'd finished, it looked more like Grace had been caught in a fight with her lost Coronet Crimson than working with a brush and comb.

"It'll have to do," she sighed, flopping down on her bed and pulling so hard on her pink ballet tights that her toes ripped right through the other end. Just when she thought things couldn't get any worse, Scarlet pirouetted perfectly across the dormitory and clapped her hands.

"Today's the day we get to choose what sort of flower we want to be in the ballet show," she said excitedly.

"Perfect," groaned Grace. She had no idea what flower she should be. . . Not many flowers grew in Cragland, and she hardly knew the difference between a rose and a dandelion.

But just at that moment, sporty Princess Latisha came dashing in to Sky Dorm.

"Stop! Change out of your ballet outfits," she said. "Madame Lightfeather has sent a message that we should come to class in our riding clothes. We have to bring our notebooks too. We're going out and about on the island."

"Really?" Grace tripped over the end of her bed as she bounded to her feet. "We're riding our unicorns instead of ballet class?" For the first time in two days a big grin spread across her face.

Madame Lightfeather reminded Grace of a flamingo. She was often dressed in pale pink and was nearly always balanced on one long, thin leg. She looked totally out of place and a little nervous standing in the stable yard as the unicorns jostled to get to the gate.

"Young Majesties," she squealed, springing backwards as Billy tried to nibble the edge of her tutu. "At this time of year, Coronet Island is home to many beautiful spring flowers. I want you to ride out in search of the one you would like to represent in the ballet show."

Grace's heart jumped. She still couldn't quite believe they were going to go for a ride instead of having the Monday morning lesson at school.

"But what about the big scary dragon Grace saw?" gulped Precious, pretending to tremble and bite her nails. "Surely it might eat us alive, Oh, but I forgot – Grace made it up!"

Grace turned Billy's head away, ignoring her cousin. There was a ripple of laughter, probably from the twins, but Grace didn't look round to see. Precious had made sure the whole class knew that the beautiful invitations for The Ballet of the Flowers had been ruined and that it was all Grace's fault. Most of them were furious with her . . . especially since they heard she'd fallen out with Scarlet and Izumi over the whole thing.

"On your ride, I want you each to pick a sample of the flower you would like to be and press it in your notebooks," said Madame Lightfeather. "However, if your flower is very rare, with less than five blooms growing in one place, please do not pick it. Make a detailed sketch and return with that instead."

"Come on," said Grace, squeezing Billy's sides with her heels. "Let's go."

But she was right at the front, and

Madame Lightfeather asked her to wait and hold open the gate for the rest of the class.

"Girls," called Precious, barging forward to ride with Scarlet and Izumi. "Let's stick together and be partners."

"All right. But we should wait for Grace too," said Scarlet.

"Really?" Precious smirked. "She might make us all gallop off the edge of a cliff or something."

"Forget it! I'd rather ride by myself," snapped Grace, too proud to tag along with her cousin while she treated Scarlet and Izumi like her new best friends.

"Never mind, then," said Scarlet. Grace saw a look of hurt flash across her face as she turned her unicorn's head and trotted away behind Precious. "If you want to sulk, I can't stop you."

Grace could have kicked herself. She

realized, too late, that although she'd meant to hurt Precious, she'd hurt Scarlet instead. Her friend had been trying to mend the silly argument and make peace. Grace had thrown that right back in her face. Even from gentle Scarlet, that might be the last chance she would get.

By the time Grace shut the gate, the princesses had galloped off together down the beach.

CHAPTER SEVEN
Eyes in the Dark

Billy pulled on his reins, desperate to follow the other unicorns across the sand.

"No. We're going this way." Grace turned his head towards the steep, stony path that led up the cliffs. She wanted to be alone – somewhere she could forget all about Precious and the other princesses, at least for a while. "I promise I'll let you have a gallop when we reach the moors," she said, as Billy picked his way carefully between the sharp rocks.

At last, Billy scrambled to the top of the cliffs. As soon as his hooves hit the soft moss of the moors he was off.

"Yippee!" cried Grace, forgetting everything as she crouched low over Billy's neck — even that she was supposed to be looking for a flower. Her long, wild hair had fallen out of its scrappy bun; it flew out behind her hat as they galloped. While the other princesses rode side-saddle, Grace always rode Billy the way a knight would ride his charger: with one leg either side of the saddle.

"Like a stable boy," Precious sniffed. But sitting side-saddle, none of the other girls in Grace's class could ride as fast or as boldly as she could. "Whoopee!" she cheered as Billy sprung over a stream.

A minute or two later they slowed to walk, as the path narrowed again and twisted through a small, dark wood.

"Did you enjoy that?" laughed Grace, leaning forward to scratch the unicorn's ears.

But as her hand stretched out, she froze. Ahead of them, at the bend in the path, something moved. Grace peered into the darkness beneath the trees. A dark shadow crouched in the gloom. Two bright orange eyes burned like coals in a fire. Grace saw a long tail flicking back and forth.

"The dragon," she whispered, her heart hammering inside her chest – half with excitement and half with fear. "It's still on the island after all."

Before she could turn Billy round, the beast sprang forward with a low growl.

Billy reared up. Grace wished that she had a crossbow like Keeper Falcon's, so that she could loose an arrow to frighten the creature away. Or at least that she had a stone she could throw. The only thing she did have was the small gold book that she used for making notes in ballet class – the one she was supposed to draw a rare flower in.

"Shoo!" she yelled, tossing the book high over Billy's ears and hoping it would be enough to scare the beast. She couldn't even see the creature through the unicorn's mane, which flew up wildly into her face as he threw his head in the air.

"Shoo!" cried Grace again, but as Billy thumped his front legs back to the ground, she saw that it wasn't a dragon, but an enormous yellow hound, that had blocked their path. It was holding her pretty gold notebook between it's teeth and slobbering over it like a chew toy.

"Oh!" As Grace's heart stopped pounding with fear, she felt a thud of disappointment in her chest. It wasn't the dragon after all: she was no closer to proving it was real.

"Drop that right now!" Hetty, Keeper Falcon's tiny, dark-haired niece, scampered out of the trees, dressed in a ragged chequered smock and carrying a long silver horn. "Sit!" she ordered crossly and grabbed the dog by its spiky collar.

The huge hound looked up at her as if she was six feet tall, and obeyed immediately. It spat the book out, which fell to the muddy path with a damp *plop!* and a splatter of drool.

Oh dear, thought Grace. *That's going to cause trouble later.* Madame Lightfeather always insisted they wrote notes about every new dance move they learned. But it was hopeless to try and rescue the book now. It was so chewed and wet that it looked like a shapeless bath sponge lying in a big puddle of dog dribble.

"Oh, Your Majesty, I'm so sorry about your pretty little book," said Hetty, darting forward to grab the soggy pages.

Grace shook her head. "Don't worry. I think it's too late to save it."

"You're a very naughty boy, Flump," said Hetty, as the dog rolled over and waited to have its tummy tickled.

"Flump? What a funny name for a great big hound like that," laughed Grace.

"Yes, Your Majesty," curtsied Hetty, as the enormous beast tried to lick the end of her nose. "He's a dragon hound. His mother and father are called Fire and Flame. But he just wouldn't suit a name like that. He's supposed to fierce and fearless, but he's a big softie, I'm afraid."

"I think he's gorgeous," said Grace.

"Me too, Your Majesty. But Uncle Falcon says he is going to send him to the mainland if he doesn't shape up," sighed Hetty. "Dragon hounds aren't meant to be too tame, you see – it makes them useless if they ever have to actually fight a dragon."

"I see," said Grace, though she wondered why the keeper was worried if he was so sure there were no dragons left on the island.

The big dog flopped to the ground at Hetty's feet. "Ever since he was a tiny puppy he's always loved rolling over to have his tummy tickled," she explained. "That's why I named him Flump. It's sort of stuck."

"Is it all right if I tickle him too?" asked Grace, swinging her feet out of the stirrups and jumping down.

"Of course." Hetty nodded. "I'm sorry if he startled you earlier. I think he was more scared than you were. He's a big baby, really."

"It was my fault for being so silly," said Grace, tickling the enormous dog as he waved his huge, hairy legs in the air like an upturned spider. "It was dark under the trees and when I saw his orange eyes . . . well, I was sure he was a dragon."

She blushed, realizing how silly Hetty must think she was.

"I suppose you heard I thought I saw a Coronet Crimson on the cliffs the other day?"

"Yes, Your Majesty. That's why I am out exploring with Flump – not that he'd be much use – but I've got this as well," said

Hetty, pointing to the silver trumpet. "I sneaked it out of Uncle Falcon's cottage. It's an ancient dragon horn. It's supposed to calm them down if you blow it."

Grace looked up to see if the little girl was laughing at her. But Hetty's eyes were wide with excitement.

"I wish I'd been there, Your Majesty," she said. "It must have been amazing to see a real dragon flying right over your head."

"So you really do believe me?" said Grace. "Even though your uncle thinks I am wrong?"

"Of course I believe you." Hetty shrugged. "It would be hard to imagine a thing like that, Your Majesty. Especially if it really was as big as a flying rhinoceros."

Grace smiled. She felt as if a boulder had slipped from her shoulders. Hetty might not be much bigger than her little sister Pip, but at least she believed what Grace had seen.

"You don't have to call me Your Majesty, by the way," she laughed. "I'm just Grace."

"Thank you," Hetty curtsied. "Although my uncle wouldn't like that. He's very strict."

Grace smiled kindly. She wasn't surprised the little girl was so afraid of the stern gamekeeper. She was about to tell her she didn't have to curtsy either, when she saw that Hetty's eyes were fixed on Billy. It was as if he was the most wonderful creature she had ever seen.

"Would you like a ride?" asked Grace. There was still time before she had to find her silly flower.

"Oh, no," gasped Hetty. "I couldn't do that."

"You're not scared of unicorns, are you?" said Grace. It didn't seem to fit with the way Hetty rolled around with Flump or scampered through the trees like a monkey. "Come on."

Grace led Billy out on to a scrubby moor on the other side of the trees. He bent his head to nibble a bunch of ragged yellowy-brown flowers like an old yak in a hayfield.

"See? He's a big softie, just like Flump," said Grace.

But Hetty still hung back.

"I am *not* scared of Billy – not even a tiny bit," she said, jutting out her chin and glaring at Grace for even suggesting such a thing. "It's just that I'm not allowed. Surely you know that. Only a princess is ever allowed to ride a unicorn."

Grace's mouth fell open. "Really? But that's stupid!" There were still so many things Grace didn't know about royal rules and customs, and so many of the things she had learned didn't seem fair or right.

"Well, Billy's *my* unicorn," she said. "And I give you permission. In fact, I insist by *royal order* that you have a ride right now!"

"Are you sure, Your Majesty – I mean, Grace?" Hetty was jiggling from one foot to the other with excitement.

"Of course I'm sure. *Royally* sure!" said Grace, taking Hetty's silver dragon horn and resting it against a tree. Why should princesses get to keep unicorns all to themselves? It was the silliest thing she'd ever heard.

"Just as long as my uncle doesn't see me," said Hetty, as she tried on Grace's riding hat and tightened the strap.

"Or my cousin, Precious," smiled Grace, holding Billy's stirrup and helping Hetty into the saddle.

"I've dreamed my whole life of riding a unicorn," beamed the little girl.

"You're going to love it," grinned Grace.

CHAPTER EIGHT
The Little White Unicorn

Grace clipped Flump's lead to Billy's bridle and led Hetty up and down the sandy track at the top of the moors. First they walked. Then they trotted. Flump bounded after them, wagging his tail.

"Oh, Grace," gasped Hetty (who had at long last stopped calling her Your Majesty). "This is brilliant. I wish I could ride a unicorn every day."

"You can," said Grace. "Or, at least, you can every day that I'm free. All we need is some nice flat grass and I'll have you cantering in no time!"

"Cantering?" Hetty nearly fell out the side of the saddle.

"You're a natural!" said Grace.

But suddenly Hetty put a finger to her lips.

"Look," she whispered, pointing to some rustling bracken at the side of the path. "We've got company."

A white unicorn foal stepped forward, his horn no bigger than a bump on his head.

"Oh!" sighed both the girls at once.

Billy whinnied. Hetty slid out of the saddle to grab hold of Flump.

"I've never seen a unicorn foal before," said Grace as they stood as still and quiet as they could.

"There are always foals on Coronet Island

in spring," whispered Hetty. "But I've never seen one so white before."

She knelt gently and pulled up a scrap of dry grass. "Here, Chalky," she whispered, beckoning to the foal. Then she put her hand to her mouth and gasped.

"Oh, dear. I shouldn't have given him a name. My uncle has always told me that."

Hetty's big, brown eyes were worried again. "You know how it works," she said. "Each First Year princess gets to name her own unicorn when she chooses it to belong to her."

It was true. Grace would never forget how she had waited for Billy to come out of the dark Jade Forest on her very first day at Tall Towers. All the other princesses had been paired with their unicorns right away, but it had seemed to take for ever until, at last, the shaggy black-and-white unicorn had decided to appear. Grace had named him Billy because he looked so much like a funny, hairy billy goat, peering out at her from under his flowing mane.

"You're wrong about one thing, though," Grace said, turning quietly towards Hetty. "A princess doesn't choose the unicorn – the unicorn chooses her."

She stroked Billy's nose and smiled at the memory of how her heart had felt that it would burst with joy when he first trotted towards her.

"It doesn't matter, anyway," said Hetty, shrugging her shoulders and sticking out her lip in exactly the same way that Pip did when she was about to cry. "You've already got Billy, and I'm never going to have a unicorn of my own, so I can't name this one, even if I want to."

"I'm not so sure about that," said Grace. "Look."

The little foal had skittered forward and was heading straight for Hetty. Very gently, he stretched out his snow-white muzzle and sniffed her hand.

"Hello there, Chalky," smiled the little girl. Then she threw up her hands. "Oh dear! I did it again."

"Careful! You'll frighten him," cried Grace. But it was too late. Chalky turned and galloped away, kicking up the sandy soil as he fled across the moor.

"I didn't mean to scare him," said Hetty, tears pricking the corner of her eyes. "But I shouldn't have given him a name. It was wrong. Giving something a name is like saying it belongs to you," she sniffed.

"I promise I won't tell anyone. Not if you don't want me to," said Grace.

"Thank you!" Hetty blushed bright red and flung her arms around Grace's neck. She blushed even more when her stomach gurgled loudly.

"Sorry," she giggled. "I think it must be—"

"Lunchtime!" cried Grace, remembering why she was out here in the first place. "I should have been back at school ages ago."

She flung the reins back over Billy's head.

"I am supposed to have chosen a flower to be for the dance," she groaned, looking across the scraggy moorland. There was nothing up here except thorn bushes and moss.

"How about some dragon's heart?" suggested Hetty.

"What a funny name. . . Is it pretty?" asked Grace.

"Not *really*," smiled Hetty. "But it is the only thing that grows up here." She pointed back towards the yellow–brown flowers that Billy had eaten when they came out of the wood. There were hundreds of them growing like nettles all along the edge of the trees.

"You're brilliant!" cried Grace, snapping off a single stem. At least there were lots and lots of them so she wouldn't have to make a sketch. There was no time, even if she had been good at drawing. And, thanks to Flump, she didn't have a book to draw in anyway. "I'd have been in such trouble if I had come back without a flower."

"Can we meet again soon and go on a dragon hunt?" grinned Hetty.

Grace was sure the Coronet Crimson was long gone but she could have hugged the little girl all over again for believing her.

"You bet!" she said. "And you can ride Billy whenever you like."

She swung her leg over the saddle and trotted away.

"There's one thing you ought to know," Hetty called after her. "When dragon's heart flowers are dry they smell like. . .

But it was too late. Hetty's voice was lost on the wind.

CHAPTER NINE
Dragon's Heart

"Poo!" Precious stood in the middle of the ballet studio holding her nose. "Somebody's flower smells *horrible!*" She coughed, pirouetted and stared straight at Grace. "I bet it's you making that dreadful smell, Cousin. After all, you do look like you've ridden through a swamp."

"I've been up on the moors, actually," Grace blushed. Everyone else had left enough time to change into their ballet clothes, but Grace was still wearing her riding habit. It was splattered with Flump's huge, muddy paw prints. And, she had to admit, her dragon's heart flower really did *not* smell very nice. In fact, it wasn't much of a flower at all – just some frayed, curly leaves and a few strips of ragged yellow-brown petal.

"Right, Class," said Madame Lightfeather, springing through the door. "Let's see what beautiful flowers you are all going to be." She stopped in mid-spin and wrinkled her nose. "Whatever is that smell? It smells like. . ."

The princesses snickered – all except Grace, who blushed as red as the beautiful poppy Scarlet was holding.

"Why are you still in your riding clothes, Grace?" asked Madame Lightfeather. "You cannot dance in that heavy coat. Go and take those muddy boots off, at least."

"Yes, Madame." Grace went to tug off her riding boots on the steps outside.

She joined the back of the line as the other princesses began to show the class their flowers. The twins had pink- and peach-coloured tulips, super-rich Princess Visalotta had a yellow crocus so bright it looked as if it was made from solid gold, and Scarlet was holding up her fragile poppy.

"Why have you chosen this one, my dear?" asked Madame Lightfeather as Scarlet pirouetted.

"I love how red it is and how delicate the petals are," said Scarlet in her clear, quiet voice. "It is almost as if they are made of tissue paper, I think."

'Lovely," Madame Lightfeather beamed. "I know you will do a wonderfully graceful dance to represent it, Scarlet."

It was Izumi next. She had drawn a beautiful, detailed sketch of a rare water lily found only in the silver lake outside the ballet studio. "I want to try and get a feeling of water in my dance," she said.

"Wonderful." Madame Lightfeather stretched, more like a beautiful bird than ever, as she explained to Izumi, "You need your arms and legs to flow like a stream."

Grace was trying to concentrate, but while four more princesses took their turn, she found it hard to focus on the class. The terrible pong from her dragon's heart flower kept wafting up her nose. She was sneezing and sniffing and her eyes were streaming too. The other princesses kept glancing over at her. Most of them were holding their noses.

"Wait" said Madame Lightfeather, just as Precious was about to step up and take her turn. "I think I'd better see Princess Grace next so that she can take her plant outside before we all faint from the smell."

"Oh . . . er . . . right. This is called dragon's heart," said Grace, stumbling forward.

"Dragon's *fart*, more like," hissed Precious. The whole class collapsed in fits of giggles. Grace knew she would probably have laughed too – if she hadn't been the one holding the stinky flower. Precious was right: that's *exactly* what it smelled like.

"Young Majesties," cried Madame Lightfeather, lifting her hands so that her long sleeves fluttered like wings. "This is not a ladylike way to behave. I am sure Princess Grace has chosen this flower for a reason. I am sure she will have some . . . well, some very *interesting* ideas for her dance."

"Ha! It looks like a weed to me," laughed Precious. Most of the class collapsed into giggles again.

"Perhaps you would like to change it for something else. A blossom maybe?" said Madame Lightfeather.

Grace shook her head. She really didn't see herself as a blossom.

"A nodding daffodil? Or a delicate pansy?" suggested the teacher.

"No, thank you." Grace looked down at her muddy riding habit and her long feet, with one toe poking out the end of her sock. "This whole class thinks I'm as scruffy as a weed anyway, and they're probably right," she sighed. "I'll stick with my dragon's heart and do the best I can to come up with some sort of dance."

"Lovely. We'll look forward to that very much," said Madame Lightfeather, although she didn't sound at all sure. "Perhaps for now, though, you could take the plant outside. And Princesses Trinket and Truffle, open the windows and let some air in."

"My turn now," said Precious, pushing forward with a black-and-yellow flower shaped like a snake's forked tongue. "At least this plant is not a weed. My dance is going to be very powerful," Precious announced. But as Grace turned to the door, she heard Madame Lightfeather scream. "Drop that at once, Princess Precious!" she warned. "Nobody touch it. That flower is called Serpent Nightshade . . . and it is deadly poisonous."

Trust Precious to choose a poisonous flower, thought Grace, feeling a little better as she stamped her feet into her muddy riding boots once more. *At least my dragon's heart won't kill anyone. Not unless they die from the pong. . .*

CHAPTER TEN
Finding a Dance

All the rest of that week, Grace tried her best to think of a way to represent her smelly, scruffy dragon's heart weed in a dance.

"Study your flowers for ideas, my dear princesses," cried Madame Lightfeather. She looked like a gleaming hummingbird today, in a flowing ballet skirt that shimmered in every shade of the rainbow. "My outfit is inspired by the colourful petals around me," she said, buzzing amongst the princesses and leaping from one girl to the next.

Most of the class had brought their flowers along to the lesson with them so that they could look closely at the pretty petals and buds – only Grace's pongy weed and Precious's poisonous nightshade were banned from being anywhere near the ballet studio ever again. "Following the little *mishap* with our invitations," said Madame, "new ones have now been sent out, along with a programme listing the flower that each princess will represent in her dance."

"I wonder if they'll write dragon's *fart* on the programme," whispered Precious, who was practicing the splits.

Grace stared down at her feet, but could tell that the whole class was looking at her. They were well aware of whose fault the little "*mishap*" had been. She had barely spoken to Izumi and Scarlet since the argument in the library, but she knew they'd spent hours making new invitations to replace the ones that she had ruined in the mud. Lots of the other princesses had helped out. But no one had asked Grace to join in.

"The show will be upon us before we know it," said Madame Lightfeather, clapping her hands excitedly. "We have a great deal of work to do, so find yourselves a partner. I want you to show each other your dance so far."

Grace didn't move. She had already seen Izumi grab Scarlet's hand. Precious had dived across the room to be partners with wealthy Visalotta. The twins were together. And best friends Princess Rosamond and Juliette, Christabel and Emmeline, Latisha and Martine had paired up too. There were only ever supposed to be twelve princesses in a class at Tall Towers. When the headmistress, Lady DuLac, had allowed Grace to join, she was number thirteen. That meant there was an odd number, so someone was left without a partner. It had never mattered before. Scarlet, Izumi and Grace had always joined together as a threesome. Grace longed to join them now.

"Hurry and find a group, my dear," said Madame Lightfeather, seeing that Grace was still alone. "I am sure one of these pairs won't mind."

But Grace shook her head. "I haven't really got much of a dance to show anybody yet," she said. "Can I practise a bit more on my own?" She pointed to the back wall of the ballet studio, which was covered from floor to ceiling in mirrors.

"Very well, if you think that's how

your ideas will blossom," said Madame Lightfeather. "But there are only three weeks until the show. You need to come up with a beautiful, creative idea for your dance very soon."

Grace nodded and stamped her feet, trying to imagine that her long legs and knobbly knees were roots pushing down into the soil. But when she stared at her reflection, she saw that all that jiggling about just made it look as if she was desperate to go to the toilet.

If only ballet didn't have to be so elegant, she thought, watching in the mirror as Princess Christabel rose up gently on her toes. Even without the white tutu she would wear for the performance, it was easy to imagine Christabel as a delicate snowdrop peeping up through the frozen ground.

Scarlet spun silently past too, her arms as

light as petals. It was as if she was a delicate stem blowing in the wind. Izumi followed, her fingers trembling like a water lily leaf on a lake.

"This is hopeless," groaned Grace under her breath. She imagined Scarlet dressed as a bright red poppy and Izumi in pale water lily-pink. "What will I wear?" she mumbled. "A piece of smelly old sack?"

Even Precious's poison-plant dance was taking shape as she spun across the room with her nose in the air, as haughty and beautiful as an evil queen.

"Search deep inside your own heart," said Madame Featherlight, lifting Grace's hands gently into the air. "You will begin to feel the dance growing inside you. You are full of imagination, my dear. I know you will come up with a wonderful idea, all in good time."

"I'll try my very best," said Grace. At that moment, she wished more than anything that she could prove her wonderful, encouraging ballet teacher right. She promised herself that she would spend the whole weekend dancing.

The trouble was, she had promised Hetty that she could ride Billy again too. . .

CHAPTER ELEVEN
Answering Back

The next morning, Grace saddled Billy and led him along the driveway to meet Hetty by the school gates.

"Watch out for Flump!" cried Hetty. Grace saw a flash of yellow out of the corner of her eye as the enormous dragon hound came bounding forward. He threw his giant paws around Grace's neck, almost knocking her to the ground, as great dribbles of drool splashed on her shoulder.

"Sorry," said Hetty. "He needs a good

run on the moors."

"I think Billy feels the same way," smiled Grace, as the shaggy unicorn shook his head and rattled the bit in his mouth. "Ready?" Grace put a twist in Billy's stirrup leathers so that they were short enough for the little girl to use. "Jump on!"

But Hetty shook her head. "It's not safe for me to ride a unicorn so close to school," she whispered. "Someone will see us."

"Perhaps you're right," agreed Grace, as she spotted Precious and the twins peering at them over the garden hedge.

"How hilarious. Grace has made friends with a scruffy servant girl," laughed Precious loudly.

"A scruffy servant! Hilarious," snorted the twins.

"Don't pay any attention to them," said Grace.

But Precious was having fun now.

"I'm not surprised Grace's only friend is a servant. She's never behaved like a *proper* princess, and now she's gone totally wild," she said, roaring with laughter. "There's not a single princess in the class who'd dare go anywhere near her. She might kick a stone at them or knock them over in the mud."

"Oh, be quiet, Precious," snapped Grace.

"Go and put a frog in your mouth. I'd be friends with Hetty no matter what. She's worth ten of you."

Flump raised his hackles and growled.

"Yes. Go and put a frog in your mouth, Princess Precious!" echoed Hetty, as she stepped out from behind Billy.

Grace thought she might explode with laughter as she turned to see the little girl with her hands on her hips. It was so good to hear someone stand up to Precious for once. Especially someone half her size! She wanted to lift Hetty up in the air and cheer.

But a second later she saw the flush of colour drain from Hetty's cheeks as she realized what she had done. And one look at Precious's furious face told Grace that it would have been better if Hetty had kept quiet.

"I am s-s-so sorry, Your Majesty," trembled Hetty, peering out from under her long, dark lashes.

"How dare you!" gasped Precious. She clutched her chest and stumbled as if she might faint. Trinket and Truffle grabbed her arms.

"A servant girl talking to *me* like *that*," breathed Precious.

"It was only a joke," said Grace. "Hetty was just copying me."

"Forgive me, Your Majesty," Hetty blushed. She bobbed down into a low curtsy, her lip wobbling as if she was about to cry.

"She didn't say anything you didn't deserve," said Grace, putting her arm around Hetty's shoulder. "You were being a horrible snob, Precious, and you know it."

She took hold of Billy's bridle and, gently

turned Hetty around. "Come on," she said. "You can help me muck out the stable if you like."

She didn't dare let Precious know they were really going for a ride – *on a unicorn*. That would be the last straw.

"You haven't heard the end of this, Hetty Falcon. Just you wait!" shouted Precious as they led Billy away. "I'll make sure you are fired from your little job feeding the peacocks. And I'll see that your uncle loses his job as gamekeeper too."

"She can't do that, can she?" gasped Hetty.

"Of course not," said Grace quickly. "Lady DuLac would never let it happen. Precious has no power over who works at Tall Towers and who doesn't." But Grace knew that Precious would find some way to make Hetty pay for what she had done.

"Even if he doesn't lose his job, Uncle

Falcon will be furious when he hears I stuck my tongue out at a real princess," shivered Hetty.

She looked more afraid than ever. Grace remembered how long it had taken Hetty to stop curtsying and calling her 'Young Majesty' when they first met. Keeper Falcon was a stern man. He had trained Hetty to be polite to every princess.

"Precious was looking for trouble. I'll happily tell that to your uncle and anyone else who wants to know," said Grace, desperate to calm Hetty's fears. "For now, we'd better try to find somewhere extra-specially secret to ride. I don't trust Precious not to follow us and see what we're up to."

"We could always go to the Gemstone Glade," said Hetty shyly. "If you really are sure you don't mind letting me have another go."

"Of course I'm sure. I'm going to teach you to canter today," said Grace. "But where's the Gemstone Glade? I've never heard of it before."

"It's a big meadow hidden in the Far Forest," said Hetty, her eyes lighting up. "It could be like a secret riding school."

"Sounds perfect," whooped Grace. "Lead the way!"

CHAPTER TWELVE
The Gemstone Meadow

Hetty rode ahead, steering Billy down a track that twisted deep into the woods. The silver dragon horn was slung over her back on a leather strap.

"I've ridden this way a hundred times," panted Grace, jogging to keep up with the unicorn and his little rider, as Flump bounded along beside them. "I thought the path just led to the cliffs."

"I told you, the Gemstone Glade is secret," said Hetty, as they left the main path and ducked into the trees. "The Tall Towers pupils forget about it because they only ever come here once a year."

Grace was about to ask why the princesses came at all. But as they reached the glade, the words caught in her throat.

"It's beautiful," she gasped.

They were standing beside a large circle of soft grass – the perfect place for Hetty to learn to canter. All around the edge of grass, like a band of jewels around a crown, was a bright ring of hundreds and hundreds of wild flowers.

"No wonder they call it the Gemstone Glade," said Grace. In the warm sun, the small, bright flowers looked like rubies and emeralds, sapphires, diamonds and pearls.

"They only bloom for a few weeks every spring," said Hetty. "But I think that makes it more special, as though it's magic."

"And not a dragon's heart weed anywhere," laughed Grace. "I should have come here when I was looking for my ballet flower."

Billy pulled hard on the reins. Hetty almost toppled over his head as he stretched down to eat a bunch of the pretty flowers.

"Oh no you don't!" Grace led Billy down to the circle of plain grass, where he could do no harm. "Let him have a bite or two here," she said, as Hetty loosened the reins and held the front of the saddle. Billy swished his tail and chewed happily.

Only Flump didn't seem to like the magical glade much. Having run twice around the edge of the ring, he stopped at the furthest edge and shivered like a frightened deer. *AWOOOO!* He threw his huge, hairy head in the air and howled.

"What's the matter with him?" asked Grace. "He sounds scared."

"I'm not sure,' said Hetty. "But you know what a baby he is."

Flump sniffed among the flowers with his bottom high in the air and his nose low to the ground. His tail was clamped tight between his legs.

"He really doesn't like the smell of something," said Grace.

"Perhaps it's all these flowers," laughed Hetty. "But he's probably just looking for food." She whistled and the huge dog came bounding towards them. "You can have something to eat in a minute. I brought cinnamon buns – I know they're your favourite."

"First we have teach you to canter, Hetty," said Grace, nearly falling over as Flump wound himself between her legs. "That means it's time for Billy to stop thinking about eating too."

She showed Hetty how to trot in a circle and then squeeze her legs so that the unicorn rocked forward and cantered gently around the ring.

"You're doing it," cried Grace. "I told you you'd be a natural."

Grace even taught the younger girl how to do a figure of eight and crisscross the ring without breaking Billy's stride. Then she had a quick canter herself – she just couldn't resist having a go on the soft green grass – before they loosened Billy's girth and let him have a proper rest.

Hetty lifted the silver dragon horn and peered inside. "I thought we might get hungry," she explained rolling up her sleeves. "So I brought some homemade elderflower cordial." She produced a green glass bottle, wrapped in a soft cloth, from deep inside the horn. "And I baked some cinnamon buns too."

"You baked these?" asked Grace, licking the sugar from her lips as she took a bite of the soft bun.

"Yes," blushed Hetty. "It's easy, really. I do

a lot of cooking because . . . well, because since my mum died, I've lived with Uncle Falcon on my own."

"What about your dad?" asked Grace, gently. "Where is he?"

"I don't even know who my dad is," shrugged Hetty. "I think he was a sailor. Or maybe a pirate." Her eyes sparkled for a second, but then a cloud passed over her face again. Hetty sniffed as she told Grace how her mum had drowned two years ago when her fishing boat had been caught in a storm at sea. "Mum always said she would tell me who my Dad was when I was older. But now I'll never know. Uncle Falcon refuses to even talk about it."

Grace held Hetty's hand and told her how she had lost her mother too. The girls talked and talked.

"Look," said Hetty. "Chalky has come back."

Sure enough, the little white unicorn was staring at them from the edge of the trees.

Billy, who was still eating grass, raised his head and whinnied.

"And there's his mum," said Grace, who could just make out the dapple-grey shape of a unicorn mare further back in the gloom.

Hetty grinned, showing the big gap where she was missing a tooth. "I thought perhaps he was like us," she said. "I thought perhaps. . ."

"Perhaps he didn't have a mummy?" asked Grace, squeezing the little girl's hand. "But he does. Look."

"Yes," Hetty peered into the trees, still grinning, then sprang suddenly to her feet. "Where's Flump?" she asked. "He didn't even come for the cinnamon buns. That's not like him at all."

There was no sign of the dog anywhere.

"Flump!" called Grace, jumping up too, and shouting as loudly as she could.

"Flump!" hollered Hetty. "Where are you?"

Chalky started at the sound of their voices, and crashed away through the trees after his mother.

"Let's tie Billy somewhere safe," said Grace. "We'll search all around. Flump can't have gone far."

Hetty nodded. "He's probably just scared himself somehow."

Awoooooo! The girls froze as the air was filled with a frightened howl.

"That's him!" cried Hetty.

Grace was already running towards the sound.

CHAPTER THIRTEEN
Behind the Ivy

Awoooooo! Flump howled again.

"I'm coming!" shouted Grace. She dashed towards a hill that rose up behind the woods on the far side of the glade, sure that was where Flump's cries were coming from. At the foot of the slope, almost hidden by the trees, she could see a long, steep ridge of rock covered in hanging ivy and vines.

Awoooooooooo!

"Perhaps he's been hurt," said Grace.

Wherever Flump was, the poor thing was in a terrible state – she could imagine the look of panic in his big, goofy eyes.

Awoooooooooooooo! Awooooooooooooooooooooo!

"That's odd." Grace skidded to a stop with Hetty just behind her. "It sounds as if he's *inside* the rock." She stretched out her hands. At first she touched a solid wall of stone . . . but suddenly her fingers passed clean through the curtain of hanging ivy.

"There's a cave behind here," she gasped, lifting the vines and peering into the gloomy darkness beyond. She could just make out the shadow of a low ceiling and sharp jagged boulders on the floor.

Awoooooooooo! Flump howled again. It was definitely coming from deep inside the cave.

"Poor thing. He sounds so scared," said Hetty.

"He must be trapped in here somewhere," said Grace edging into the gloom. "You stay in the glade with Billy. I'll go and find him."

Grace didn't wait for Hetty to answer. She pushed aside a spider's web and plunged into the darkness. Her heart was beating fast. She had to rescue the big, silly dog before he scared himself to death.

"I'm coming, Flump!" she called, boldly.

There was a scrabble of stones behind her.

"Who's there?" Grace jumped, almost banging her head on the low ceiling of the cave.

"Only me," said a tiny voice. Hetty grabbed Grace's hand. "I'm coming too," she said. "Billy will be all right. I tied him to a tree with the special safety knot you taught me."

"You'd be much safer to wait outside," said Grace. "Then you could run for help if. . ."

"Next you're going to tell me I'm too little," Hetty growled. "Well, I'm not." She stood on tiptoes so the top of her head *almost* reached Grace's shoulder. "I have to help find Flump. He hates it when I'm not around."

Grace smiled to herself in the darkness. Hetty reminded her so much of her little sister, Princess Pip. They might be small, but they were very brave, and once they set their mind to something there was no point in trying to argue.

Grace couldn't be cross; she knew she would feel exactly the same if it was Billy who was in danger. "Keep hold of me tight and be very careful, then," she sighed.

Awoooooooo!

They followed Flump's howls deeper and deeper into the gloom. There was just enough light to see that the cave was lined with rows of spikey rocks, sharp as teeth, pushing up from the floor, and hanging down from the ceiling too.

"Yikes! It's like we're standing inside a dragon's mouth," trembled Hetty.

"As long as that's not dragon spit," said Grace, as drips of water splashed on to their heads from the damp roof above.

They picked their way over the stony floor until the ceiling sloped so low that Grace could hardly stand up. She stretched out her hand and felt a cold, slimy wall of rock. She ran her fingers from side to side, feeling up and down.

"It's the end of the cave," she said. "But that's impossible. Flump must be in here somewhere. We heard him so clearly."

"What's that?" Hetty pointed to a dim shaft of light no brighter than a candle, flickering between two of the huge tooth-like rocks.

Awooooooo! Flump howled again. The sound was definitely coming from the same direction as the light.

"Don't let go of me," Grace warned as they scrambled forward.

The glow was brighter now. Grace saw that the light was coming through a narrow slit in the wall.

"Daylight," she gasped, as she glimpsed a thin sliver of blue sky. There was a smell of salt and the sound of waves crashing far below.

"I think this is a back entrance to the cave," said Grace, peering through the slit which was like a arrow hole in a castle wall. "It must come out somewhere on the cliffs."

She ducked her head, to see if she could squeeze through.

Awoooooooooo!

"Flump?" Hetty pushed Grace out of the way and tried to wriggle through the gap first. There was no doubt about it, the dog's anxious howls were definitely coming from just the other side of the crack.

"Stop!" Grace grabbed the back of Hetty's smock. "Don't take another step," she whispered urgently. "Look."

Grace pointed with a shaking finger as three puffs of grey smoke floated through the gap towards them.

Awooooooooooooooooo! Flump howled from the ledge outside.

Huffffffff. More smoke billowed through the crack.

"A dragon," cried the girls together.

CHAPTER FOURTEEN
Saving Flump

"How are we going to save Flump now?" wailed Hetty as the girls stood quivering in the cave. They couldn't see anything through the narrow gap in the rock, but there was no doubt there was a dragon out there.

"The Coronet Crimson must have stayed on the island after all," gulped Grace.

"Now she's got Flump and she's going to eat him," bawled Hetty. "Oh, why didn't anyone believe you when you said you'd seen a dragon, Grace?"

The little girl dashed forward as if she was going to squeeze through the gap and punch the dragon right on the end of its fiery nose.

"Don't. She'll gobble you up in one bite," cried Grace, trying to grab Hetty. She caught hold of the horn, which was still strapped to the little girl's back.

"Of course!" said Grace. "Isn't this thing supposed to calm dragons down?"

"I think so," said Hetty, her feet almost dangling in the air as Grace pulled her backwards with the horn.

"It has to be worth a try," said Grace, hooking the instrument around her own neck. "I'm going to peek through the gap and see what's going on. If I can rescue Flump, I will."

"You're not like other princesses," whispered Hetty. "Uncle Falcon said you're a disgrace . . . but that's not true. You're brilliant and brave and. . ." Hetty stood on tiptoes and kissed Grace's cheek. "And I wish you were my big sister."

Grace blushed so hard that she felt as if her face must be glowing bright red in the dark cave. "You stay well back," she said firmly, trying to sound as strict as Fairy Godmother Flint. "And if there's any trouble — any trouble at all — ride to Tall Towers and fetch help."

She smiled for a second, trying not to think about her shaking knees, as she imagined what Precious's face would look like if she saw Hetty galloping into the school courtyard on a royal unicorn shouting: "Help! We've found a dragon on the cliffs!" At least that would show her, once and for all, that Grace had been telling the truth!

It was no good, though. At the thought of the magnificent but terrifying creature she had seen the day she'd fallen out of the tree, Grace's knees began to shake all the harder. If the dragon had seemed enormous when she was flying in the sky, what would she be like face to face?

Awoooooooo!

Another smoke ring floated through the gap.

Grace's lips trembled, but she straightened her shoulders, lifted the instrument to her lips, and blew.

Nothing. Not a sound.

Grace pursed her lips and blew again, harder.

Still nothing.

She puffed out her cheeks, blew through her nose and . . . *parp*! At last the horn made a noise. But it sounded very rude – a bit

like Billy when he'd been eating too many pomegranate seeds.

"Oh dear," murmured Grace, blushing all over again. "Surely it's not meant to sound like that?"

"Of course it's not!" Hetty reached up, took the horn and blew.

Pom! Pom! Pom! The instrument at once made a bright, cheerful sound like the beginning of a dance.

"Oh, no!" Grace had hoped the horn would have some kind of special magic – something that would send the dragon to sleep.

"A tune like that is just going to make her more lively," Grace groaned.

Awoooooooo! Flump howled.

Slowly – very slowly – and without making another sound, the girls edged forward. Hetty ducked down between Grace's legs and they peered through the narrow gap in the rocks. They could see a wide stone ledge beyond, as broad as the deck of a ship.

"Look!" gasped Grace.

"Oh!" squealed Hetty.

Flump was standing on the tip of the ledge, which jutted out of the cliffs high above the sea.

Awoooooooooooo! He was shaking like a bowl of orange jelly.

Huff! A perfect ring of smoke floated into the air.

In the middle of the ledge was the dragon. . .

"But . . . it's tiny," said Grace in surprise. She edged out on to the wide ledge.

Curled in a nest of seaweed, with its bright red tail tucked under its snout, was a little crimson dragon pup no bigger than a piglet.

"Silly old Flump!" laughed Hetty, as the quivering dog darted past the dragon and threw his paws around her neck. "How could you be scared of something so small . . . and cute?"

"It's just a baby," grinned Grace.

CHAPTER FIFTEEN
Huffle

Grace stared at the tiny dragon pup. She had never seen anything so extraordinary in all her life.

"It's definitely a Coronet Crimson," she whispered.

Hetty held out her arms and Flump jumped right into them.

"Imagine being terrified of something so adorable," chuckled Hetty. "You're supposed to be a dragon hound who can fight off three-headed serpents with one snarl."

The enormous dog buried his head in his paws and whimpered.

"Look!" Grace pointed to the dragon's tiny, fluttering wings. They were fringed with gold. "The mother's wings were tipped with silver. That means he's a boy, I think."

"He's soooo cute," cooed Hetty, pushing forward.

But Grace held her back. "Wait. The mother dragon could return at any moment," she said, glancing anxiously across the ledge towards the blue sky and rolling sea. "She wouldn't leave her pup alone in the nest for long."

Huff! The little dragon opened his mouth as if to warn them away. A tiny orange spark flew into the air.

"Oh, no!" cried Grace. "He's set his nest on fire."

The dry seaweed crackled: the little dragon had breathed just one flickering spark, but it was enough. Red flames leaped up around the tiny pup.

Awooooooo, howled Flump.

The frightened dragon flapped his flimsy wings, but he was far too young to fly.

"We have to save him!" cried Grace. The little dragon looked so tiny and helpless. She dashed forward and stamped her heavy riding boots down on the growing flames, tramping in wild circles around the tiny, terrified pup. In every dance class she had ever been to, Grace had been told to land gently on her feet. But now she stomped and thumped and clumped for all she was worth.

"Behind you," cried Hetty as another flame shot up into the air.

Grace twirled and spun around quicker than she had ever been able to pirouette.

The seaweed crunched and crackled as she crashed her boot down on the last leaping flame and the fire went out.

"Well done. You saved him," cheered Hetty.

Grace, clutched her stomach, gasping for breath.

"Now, you listen to me, young Mr Huffle," said Grace, crouching down and staring into the baby dragon's big gold eyes. "Don't you go setting yourself on fire like that ever again. You frightened me half to death."

Huff! The tiny dragon puffed again, but this time there were no flames – just a ring of smoke. He edged closer to Grace, all his fear gone. He seemed to know she only wanted to help.

"The poor thing," said Grace as the little creature opened and closed his mouth like a baby bird. "I think he's hungry."

She felt the dry seaweed in the nest.

It crumbled like dead leaves beneath her fingers.

"No wonder this burned so easily," she said. "The mother dragon is supposed to keep it wet. I read about it in a book I found in the library. Dragons fly out to sea every hour or so and fetch water in their mouths to dampen the nest so that any little sparks the baby breathes won't set it on fire."

"That means the mummy dragon's gone away," said Hetty, creeping closer.

Grace looked at the singed seaweed and nodded. "This nest should be as soggy as a sponge," she said. "But it is as dry as paper. I don't think the mother dragon has been here for a very long time."

"She's abandoned him," gasped Hetty. "Why would she do that? Poor little Huffle."

"Perhaps something has happened to her,"

said Grace, as the dragon pup nibbled the hem of her riding habit. "Something that means she can't come back."

Grace looked out across the sapphire sea again. Just a few minutes earlier she had been afraid that the mother dragon would return. Now she wished that she would.

"Many dragons were lost after my uncle drove them away from Cornet Island," said Hetty. "He didn't mean for it to be like that. But smugglers came and took them from the new nest sites. They captured the dragons to sell at travelling fairs, or kept them in cages to use in fights."

Grace shuddered. "I hope that hasn't happened to the beautiful dragon I saw. She must have been Huffle's mother. If she really is the last Coronet Crimson in the world, she'd certainly be very valuable. Somebody could get a lot of money for selling such a rare creature."

Huff! the little dragon cried out again.

"But she's not the last Coronet Crimson anymore, is she?" said Grace jumping to her feet. "Not since this little fellow hatched." She pointed to bits of bright green broken egg shell at the edge of the nest.

Huff! The red pup gasped and thumped his tail on the seaweed.

"We have to look after him," said Grace. "Without his mummy he'll die."

Hetty clapped her hands in excitement. "Can he be our dragon?" she asked.

Grace wished more than anything that they could raise Huffle by themselves, but after a moment she shook her head.

"We have to fetch Keeper Falcon," she said. "He's the school gamekeeper. He'll know what we should do."

"No." Hetty grabbed Grace's hand. Her eyes were as wide and worried as Huffle's. "If we tell Uncle Falcon, he'll drive Huffle away. Just like her did with all the other dragons."

Grace remembered how Keeper Falcon had smiled when he told her he had got rid of every Coronet Crimson on the island. Grace felt her stomach twist with fear. She looked down at the tiny, helpless pup. Hetty was right. They would have to keep Huffle a secret – for the moment, at least.

"He's too small to do anyone any harm," she said. "He can't even fly off this ledge until his wings are stronger." She looked at the steep cliff face that rose above them, and the deep drop to the sea below. "The only way anyone can reach him out here is if they come through the cave."

"And no one's going to do that," said Hetty, clapping her hands again. "The entrance is hidden by all that ivy."

"And the Gemstone Glade is so secret,

nobody from Tall Towers ever goes there anyway," said Grace. "The princesses will be safe. Huffle is only a baby, and we will be the only people who come anywhere near him."

The two girls hugged in excitement, being very careful not to go anywhere near the edge of the wide ledge.

"The first thing we need to do is find Huffle something to eat," said Grace, crouching beside him. "And we'll have to keep the nest wet too."

Huff. The little dragon cried out again, but quieter this time. Weaker. He curled up in the nest, his little sides puffing up and down. It was impossible to imagine he would ever grow up to be a fierce fire-breathing beast: right now he was more like a poorly puppy.

Even Flump crept a little closer to look, his head on one side.

"Poor Huffle. He's so hungry," said Hetty. "But what does a baby dragon eat?"

"Milk!" said Grace, jumping up so fast that she almost tripped over Flump. "All babies like milk. If we feed him some of that he'll be strong again in no time."

"Where are we going to get milk from?" asked Hetty.

"Yaks?" suggested Grace.

"There aren't any yaks on Coronet Island, silly," giggled Hetty.

"Cows, then," said Grace. "There's a school dairy herd. They graze in the field behind the stables. Come on."

Grace blew a little kiss to Huffle.

"Don't worry," she said. "We'll be back here with a bucket of frothy milk in no time. I may not be very good at dancing, but I *do* know how to milk a yak . . . or a cow. I expect it works just the same way!"

"You can't do that," gasped Hetty. "You're a pupil at Tall Towers. You're royal. . . You're. . .

"A princess?" grinned Grace. "That doesn't mean I can't get my hands a tiny bit dirty!"

CHAPTER SIXTEEN
The Runaway Unicorn

The girls were so excited that they almost ran back through the cave, tripping in the darkness as they hurried towards the bright light outside.

Flump had already bolted out into the Gemstone Glade, determined to get as far away from the little dragon as he could.

"Don't worry, Huffle. We'll be back soon," Grace called over her shoulder.

Her mind was whirling like a spinning ballerina.

They had a real dragon pup to look after: a secret only she and Hetty could know about. It was just about the most brilliant thing that had ever happened to her.

"All we need to do is jump on Billy and ride to the cow pasture," she said.

But as they stepped out into the sunny glade, Hetty's face turned as white as a bucket of milk.

"But where is Billy?" she gasped. "I tied him to that tree. I know I did. I used the special safety knot you taught me."

Grace stared at the birch tree. There was no sign of Billy, just a frayed length of rope, no longer than a hair ribbon.

"I'm so sorry." Hetty's eyes filled with tears. "I really thought I tied him properly."

"I'm sure you did," smiled Grace kindly. She felt the end of the rope. It was damp and soggy. "Just as I thought. Billy's chewed right through this," she said. "There was nothing you could have done to stop him."

She glanced around the glade, but the naughty unicorn was long gone.

"He's so greedy, I'll bet he's headed back to the stable to see if there's any fresh peaches in his trough," she sighed. "Come on. We'd better find him."

They heard hooves approaching behind them and turned round. But it wasn't Billy. It was Chalky, the unicorn foal. He followed close behind Hetty, trotting to catch up whenever she walked faster.

"You really have got a friend there," laughed Grace as they hurried through the trees.

She wasn't too worried about Billy; she was sure he had just become tired of waiting and taken himself back to Tall Towers.

But as they came out of the woods, she heard someone calling on the path.

"Grace? Grace? Are you there?"

"Izumi?" Grace answered the call.

"Are you all right?" It was Scarlet shouting now. And, a moment later, Grace's friends came hurrying round the corner.

"Are you hurt?" asked Izumi.

"We were worried you'd had a fall," explained Scarlet. "Billy came charging down the drive towards school. When we saw he had no rider we thought something terrible might have happened. "

She pointed back down the track. Precious appeared, riding Billy side-saddle towards them. She was holding his reins far too tight and Billy was tossing his head furiously.

"But you didn't fall off, did you, Grace?" sneered Precious, pulling even harder so that Billy came to a stop. "You weren't even riding, were you?"

"No. Billy was tied to a tree," said Grace,

trying desperately not to mention either the Gemstone Glade or the dragon pup. "Hetty and I were just. . ."

"Having a riding lesson!" said Precious cutting right across her. "Look!"

She slid to the ground and held out the stirrup leathers. Anyone could see they were far too short for Grace's long, spindly legs.

Precious glared at Hetty. "The only person who could have needed stirrups this short is that servant child."

Hetty had risen up on tiptoes and was stretching her neck in the air just like the unicorn foal, who was still right behind her. It did nothing to make her look taller.

"I'm sure Hetty wasn't riding," said Izumi. "Only princesses are allowed to ride unicorns."

Grace threw her hands in the air. Honestly, was Izumi going to be just as snobby as Precious? She had never thought her friend would care about silly rules like that. And now Scarlet was joining in too.

"Grace *definitely* knows that nobody except a princess is *ever* allowed to ride a unicorn," she said gently.

"I didn't, actually. Not until recently," snapped Grace. Perhaps she was better off not being friends with *any* princesses if they were all going to be like this. "I think rules like that should. . ."

"Should be obeyed," said Izumi quickly. "That's what you think, isn't it Grace?" She coughed as if she had something caught in her throat.

"Oh!" Suddenly Grace understood. Scarlet and Izumi didn't think it was wrong for Hetty to have a go on Billy if she wanted to. *Of course* they didn't. Grace should have known them better than that. They just didn't want Precious to cause trouble.

"Hetty knows she isn't allowed to ride a unicorn. Don't you?" smiled Scarlet, crouching down so that she was almost the same height as the little girl.

Hetty shook her head, then nodded, then shook her head again as if she didn't know whether to tell the truth to Precious or agree with Scarlet's excuses. In the end she settled for a curtsy to both of them.

"Have you seen the lovely foal who is following her . . . I mean *us*," said Grace, pointing at Chalky to change the subject. She shot Scarlet and Izumi a quick smile of thanks.

"He's gorgeous," said Izumi. "As white as moonlight."

"And look at his cute little horn," cooed Scarlet.

"He is beautiful, isn't he?" agreed Hetty. She stretched out her hand to stroke his nose.

"Don't touch him!" shrieked Precious. At that, the unicorn turned and galloped away into the woods.

"You frightened him," cried Scarlet.

"And Billy too," said Grace, taking her own unicorn away from Precious.

"A servant has no right to even touch a unicorn," snapped Precious. "I know what you've been up to here, Grace. You and your little friend."

Grace felt her heart thud hard against her chest. Had Precious followed them? Surely she didn't know about the dragon pup? There was no way she could have found out about that.

"I know you've been giving that girl riding lessons," said Precious, waving her hand towards Hetty. "I'll find a way to prove it. Then I'll report you to Flintheart."

Grace felt her shoulders relax. Precious

had no idea about Huffle – she was still just talking about breaking silly royal rules.

"You'll probably be expelled," snarled Precious, turning on her heel and storming away down the path.

"Oh dear, I think you've upset her," smiled Izumi when Precious was out of sight.

Scarlet, who was always a terrible giggler, began to laugh.

Soon Grace was laughing too, and even Hetty joined in.

"Only a princess is allowed to ride a unicorn," mimicked Izumi, sticking her nose in the air and flicking her short black fringe so that for a moment it was possible to imagine she had Precious's long butter-yellow curls.

"Thank you both for sticking up for us," said Grace.

"That's what friends do," shrugged Scarlet. And the three of them threw their arms around each other in an enormous hug.

"I should have known you'd never be as stuck up as Precious," said Grace.

"So we're friends again?" said Izumi.

"Of course," said Grace and they hugged each other all over again.

Grace could have skipped for joy as they headed along the path towards school. She was back with her two best friends at last. Hetty was just behind them, leading Billy – she didn't dare to ride him in case Precious came back. Flump was bounding along ahead. Everything was perfect.

"So where did you have your riding lesson?" asked Izumi. "Was it somewhere top secret?"

Grace felt a cloud pass over her again.

"Oh, nowhere special," she heard herself say.

She knew Izumi would love to see the Gemstone Glade. She would be desperate to paint the beautiful flowers. But Grace couldn't risk taking her there. Not while Huffle was hidden on the ledge beyond the cave. Izumi might be happy to help break a silly, unfair rule like the one that said only princesses were allowed to ride a unicorn. But she was much more sensible than Grace. She'd be bound to report a dragon to the school – even if it was only a pup, small enough to fit into the little chest where she kept her paints.

"Yes, tell us all the fun things you two got up to," said Scarlet, smiling at Hetty and Grace.

"Nothing much," said Grace quickly. She felt the cloud hovering over her grow darker still. But she *definitely* couldn't tell Scarlet about the dragon. The red-haired princess was so nervous she'd probably run screaming right to school.

"Oh," said Scarlet.

"Right," said Izumi.

Her two friends could tell that Grace was holding something back.

"Well, I'd better take Billy to the stables," said Grace. "Hetty can help me."

She didn't want the girls to come in case they saw her trying to milk the cows. She knew she had to feed Huffle soon.

"We'll see you later," said Scarlet, sounding a little sad.

"Yes," said Grace. "Of course."

But the secret of the dragon pup was rippling inside her. As she watched Scarlet and Izumi turn towards school, it was as though she could feel the friendship drifting away again. She wanted to tell them everything.

She knew she couldn't.

She had promised she would keep that little dragon pup safe.

CHAPTER SEVENTEEN
Cows

As soon as Billy was settled safely in his stable, Hetty and Grace slipped under the fence and into the field of cows. Grace was carrying an empty water bucket.

"We can take the milk back to Huffle in this," she said.

She crept around the far side of one of the big black-and-white cows so that if anyone came down to the stables they wouldn't be able to see her.

"All right, old girl?" she said, gently

patting the cow's rump as she knelt beside her udder and began to milk.

"I never thought I'd see a princess doing this," giggled Hetty.

Grace looked at the ground. She had found a clean spot to kneel on, but there was mud and puddles all around. Not to mention worse things that the cows had left behind.

"Can you imagine if we had milking lessons for every Tall Towers princess?" laughed Grace, picturing the girls in their pretty white pinafores. "At least I wouldn't be such a terrible student then. I've had plenty of practice with the yaks at home."

Flump, who had followed them into the field, plucked up his courage and tried to sniff the end of a cow's nose.

Moo! The cow blew back at him.

Poor Flump sprang into the air and ran yelping in a wild circle.

That set the cows charging in all directions too.

"Steady," soothed Grace, patting the one she was milking. But it was hopeless. The big cow joined her friends.

"Whoa! Grab the milk, Hetty!" cried Grace, but it was too late to save herself. As the cow charged forward, Grace toppled over – *splat!* – head-first into a muddy puddle.

"Oh dear! You do look funny." Hetty was shaking so hard with laughter that milk was slopping out of the pail.

Thick, brown

mud was spattered all down the front of Grace's clothes and puddle water dripped from the end of her plaits. "Now I really am a disgrace!" she said, throwing her head back and laughing as hard as Hetty.

Flump, who was even filthier, jumped into Grace's arms for protection from the cows. "Look out!" cried Hetty. Grace toppled over backwards this time. *Splat!*

Now all of her was covered in mud.

"I look like a monster from the swamp," she groaned, standing up dripping.

"Save me, Flump!" cried Hetty pretending to be terrified and running away screaming.

"Grrr!" roared Grace, chasing her towards the gate.

But a moment later there was a real scream.

It was Precious peering out from the stable yard. "Look at the state of you," she squealed.

"Goodness, what happened?" asked Scarlet as Grace oozed and squelched her way up the stairs to their attic dormitory high in the top of the tower.

"Er. . ." Grace decided it was best to stick to the truth as much as possible, so long as she didn't have to mention a certain baby dragon. "I fell over in the cow field . . . and then Flump jumped on me," she said.

"What were you doing in the cow field in the first place?" laughed Izumi.

"Oh, nothing much," blushed Grace. This was getting harder and harder. She wished she could tell her friends the whole truth.

"I'll tell you what she was doing," said Precious, who came panting up the stairs after Grace. "She was helping that servant child to steal a bucket of milk. She's so scruffy and poor I bet she doesn't have enough to eat."

"That's terrible," said Scarlet and Izumi together.

"Yes, isn't it? The horrible little thief," crowed Precious.

"We meant it's terrible if Hetty doesn't have enough food," sighed Izumi. "Poor thing."

"It's not like that," said Grace, desperately.

"A thief is a thief," snapped Precious. "I'm going to tell Flintheart."

"Hetty wasn't stealing anything," said Grace. She shook her head so that muddy water flew off the end of her plaits in all directions and the girls had to duck. "Sorry!" she said.

"Watch what you're doing," screamed Precious, who was sprayed in the eye,

"Hetty has plenty to eat," Grace explained. The only hungry one was the poor dragon pup waiting desperately for them on the cliff. Grace thought as fast as she could.

"I was the one who wanted the milk," she said. "I . . . er . . . I heard it could make a unicorn's mane shine like moonlight. I . . . er . . . thought I'd try washing Billy and see if it was true."

"Silly thing," laughed Scarlet.

"It's not milk, it's morning dew that makes a unicorn's mane shine," smiled Izumi.

"Oh, right," said Grace. Perhaps it was a good thing after all that her friends thought she was a little hopeless. At least they were ready to believe her lie.

"Idiot," snarled Precious. "You really don't know anything do you? I'm still telling Fairy Godmother Flint. . ."

"Still telling me *what*?" said a stern voice at the door. The fairy godmother herself appeared in the room.

"Telling you that I was the one who made the mess on the stairs," said Grace, pushing forward quickly before Precious could say a word.

"I think I can see that for myself," said Flintheart, glaring down her long, thin nose at Grace, who was still dripping mud in a pool around her feet. "Get yourself cleaned up and then you can scrub the floors until they shine like marble."

"Yes, Fairy Godmother," nodded Grace.

"But. . ." began Precious.

"Out of here, the rest of you," snapped Flintheart. "You'll only make matters worse, spreading this muck and muddle everywhere. Go on. Shoo!"

Scarlet stepped forward and spoke up in a tiny voice. "Couldn't we help Grace, Fairy Godmother? Then the job would be done twice as fast."

"Certainly not!" barked Flintheart. "Grace has to learn a lesson. Real princesses do not walk around looking like pigs in a sty. If I find anyone helping her, Grace will scrub every stairway in this school."

"We're going," said Izumi, grabbing Scarlet's arm. They dashed away in a flash. Grace knew her friends were only being kind. Tall Towers had *a lot* of stairs. They would make things worse if they tried to stay.

Grace scrubbed and cleaned like a whirlwind, but it still seemed to take hours. Poor Hetty was hiding with the milk at the edge of the woods. She must be wondering where Grace had got to. But there were clods of mud on every floorboard and splashes of muck on every wall. There was even a filthy handprint right in the middle of the white dormitory door. Flintheart would never let Grace go until everything was spotlessly clean.

As she worked, all Grace could think about was poor little Huffle, who would be growing weaker by the hour as he waited desperately for his milk.

CHAPTER EIGHTEEN
Feeding Huffle

At last the job was done.

Grace bolted across the courtyard. "See you later," she shouted to Scarlet and Izumi, who were sitting together in the shade under the peach tree.

"Where are you going now?" Izumi hollered after her. "Come back! We've been waiting for you for hours."

"We thought we could do something together," Scarlet called.

"Sorry, got to go," Grace cried, wishing

more deeply than ever that she could stay with her friends — or at least tell them the truth about why she was running off.

"Suit yourself!" snapped Izumi. "I don't know what's wrong with you at the moment, Grace."

"I could have been practising my ballet," said Scarlet weakly.

Oh no — the ballet, thought Grace as she sped out of sight. She had promised to practise this weekend. Scarlet's dance was already perfect, but Grace barely had a single move, other than wobbling her arms about like a crazy scarecrow.

I'll have to practice later, she thought, dashing on. She couldn't waste another moment — she had to feed the baby dragon.

When she found Hetty, they took a side of the bucket each and hurried through the woods, trying not to spill too much more of the precious milk. They had decided to leave Billy and Flump behind this time. The poor dog had been so terrified, and Billy might try to escape again.

"It's further than I remembered," panted Hetty, as they reached the cave at last.

"We're here now, Huffle," whispered Grace, as they scrabbled through the dark and stepped out on to the hidden ledge beyond.

She had expected the little dragon to be weak and sleepy, but instead he greeted them with a furious cough of flame.

"Stop that," cried Grace. "Or you'll set your nest on fire again."

Pom! Hetty blew her horn, which she had kept hung over her back. But it didn't seem to calm the dragon down.

"Don't be angry with him," she said. "He's just hungry, that's all."

"I know how he feels," laughed Grace. "I get really cranky when I don't eat." She couldn't really be cross with the little dragon anyway – not even after all the trouble he had caused. He was just a helpless baby. He wrinkled the end of his long nose as if he could smell the milk, and stared up at Grace with hopeful golden eyes.

"There you go – get your snout in that," smiled Grace, pushing the bucket to the edge of the nest. She didn't dare go any closer in case the creature blew flames again.

"When the bucket's empty we can use it to fetch water to dampen the nest so he doesn't set it on fire," she said to Hetty. "We have to start thinking like a mother dragon now."

Huffle stood up on shaky legs. He

sniffed the milk and blew bubbles across its surface. Then he stuck his nose in the bucket, snorted, and pulled it out again, hissing steam.

"It's no good," cried Grace. "He can't drink like that. He's just a baby." She clasped her head in her hands. "I should have thought of that. We always use a bottle to feed the orphan yaks at home."

"But where are we going to get a baby bottle from?" said Hetty. "Uncle Falcon doesn't have any. He won't even feed the baby deer he finds. He says orphan creatures have to learn to look after themselves."

Hetty turned her head away, but not before Grace saw that her eyes were full of tears. She thought how terrible it must be to grow up with someone so cold and uncaring as Keeper Falcon, especially when

Hetty was an orphan herself.

"We mustn't let him find Huffle," Hetty sniffed.

The dragon blew bubbles helplessly in the bucket of milk, then wobbled and fell weakly back into the nest.

"I just wish we knew what to do," said Grace.

Pom! Pom! Pom! Hetty blew on the horn. "At least this useless old thing might cheer us all up while we try to think," she said, drying her eyes.

"Wait . . . that's brilliant." Grace grabbed the silver instrument. "This horn might be totally useless for calming dragons down, but it's perfect for feeding them."

She turned the horn around so that the wide bell-shaped end was closest to her, then pointed the narrow mouthpiece towards Huffle.

Almost straightaway, the little dragon took it in his mouth and began to suck.

"Quick," cried Grace. "Grab the bucket, Hetty. Pour a drop of milk down the end of the horn as if it is a funnel."

"Or a giant baby bottle," laughed Hetty as the little dragon sucked and drank the milk. Because he was feeding from the end of the horn, the girls could stand far enough away not to get burned even if

he did cough flames at them.

In no time at all, the bucket was empty.

"All gone," smiled Grace.

Burp! A perfect smoke ring floated through the air.

"I beg your pardon," laughed Grace. But Huffle just curled up in his nest with his tail wrapped under his chin, and fell asleep.

Soon he was snoring happily. His tummy looked fat and full, and little puffs of smoke popped out of his nostrils with every breath.

"If we can feed him like that every day, he'll be strong in no time," said Grace.

And she was right. By the end of just one week, Huffle was no longer the size of a little piglet. He had grown as big as a foal.

CHAPTER NINETEEN
In the Glade

It was often impossible for Grace to sneak away from school, especially with more and more rehearsals for the Ballet of the Flowers, but she taught Hetty how to milk a cow so that Huffle would never go hungry. As soon as she had finished feeding the peacocks and doves, Hetty went to the cave to look after the dragon.

By Saturday, Grace hadn't managed to see Huffle for three whole days.

She woke at dawn and crept out of the

dormitory before Scarlet and Izumi were awake. They would only ask her questions, and Grace hated lying to them or pretending she hadn't heard. The strain was returning to the friendship as the secret of the dragon forced her to push the girls away.

Worse still, Precious seemed to be spying on her. She was desperate to catch Grace letting Hetty ride her unicorn, but Grace began to worry that her cousin suspected her of other secrets too. If Precious ever found out about the dragon, she would call her father, and a hundred knights would come rushing from his kingdom ready to drive the creature away . . . or worse, to slay him in a fight.

Huffle might be growing fast, but he wouldn't stand a chance.

Luckily, Grace was up so early that the dormitory tower was silent and the stairs were deserted. She hurried out to the courtyard just as the bright sun peeped through the clouds. She had hidden a note for Hetty in the peacock pens with instructions to meet at the Gemstone Glade just after dawn. Grace saddled Billy and trotted out of the yard. She had decided to take him with her today. It meant she could reach the glade much quicker and the other princesses would think she had gone off for a long ride. She slung a bulging hay net over the saddle and hoped that would keep Billy happy if they had to tie him up.

She trotted all the way there, stopping just once to pick a sprig of dragon's heart, which she hoped might offer inspiration. She'd promised herself she would find time to practise her dance today, and at least the weed didn't smell quite so bad when it was in the open air and freshly picked.

Hetty was waiting on the path outside the glade. "Hello," the younger girl cried. "I can't believe we can spend the whole day with our baby dragon."

"And you can ride Billy too, of course," smiled Grace.

"Just so long as Chalky doesn't get jealous," frowned Hetty, pointing to the trees, where the little unicorn was waiting.

"He's like your shadow," laughed Grace as they entered the glade. The little foal crept after them.

Grace hung Billy's hay net from a tree. "Share that nicely with Chalky," she said firmly, before pushing through the curtain of ivy and disappearing into the cave.

Huffle wagged his tail like a dog when the girls stepped out onto the ledge. He seemed very pleased to see Grace after all this time. He rubbed his nose against her shoulder and let her scratch behind his funny, leathery ears. Now that he wasn't frightened of them, he never huffed and puffed at the girls, although they still kept the nest nice and damp just in case.

At last, when they had tickled his belly and fed him his milk, Huffle curled up for his usual morning nap.

"Come on, Hetty. You can ride Billy while Huffle rests," said Grace. "We'll come back in half an hour and see if he's woken up."

So the two girls crept back out through the cave. Hetty and Billy trotted figure of eights across the glade, with Chalky bouncing behind to keep up.

"You're getting so good at riding now," called Grace. "That's a perfect rising trot."

She stared down at the crinkled dragon's heart weed lying where she had dropped it on the grass. It didn't give her any new ideas, but she knew that while Hetty was riding she should use the time to stretch and turn. Her dance was as hopeless as ever, but she had to do something.

She spun away across the glade and gasped.

"Huffle!" The little dragon must have squeezed through the crack from the ledge. He was standing in the mouth of the cave, poking his nose out through the curtain of ivy and sniffing the air.

Slowly, he crept forward, swishing his tail across the grass.

"This will mean trouble," sighed Grace, but she couldn't help smiling as the dragon came face to face with Chalky. She thought for a moment that Huffle might be frightened and blow smoke. But it was obvious that the two young creatures just wanted to play. They rolled around like kittens, chasing and stalking and running again.

It soon turned into a game for the girls too. Hetty rode Billy alongside Chalky, and Grace stalked Huffle, copying his movements in a sort of crazy dance. She thumped her feet on the ground, mimicking the heavy way he stamped his paws, and arched her back and shook her head just like he did. She even wiggled her bottom, pretending to swish an imaginary tail.

"That looks great," laughed Hetty. "Far better than your flower dance."

"Thanks," Grace grinned. "I'm much better at stomping like a dragon pup than pretending to have petals."

"My uncle says he's seen dances in faraway countries where whole villages dress up and pretend to be a dragon," said Hetty.

"I saw a picture like that in the dragon book I found in the library," said Grace, remembering the silk costume she'd seen, with the long line of dancers and the huge dragon mask at the front.

Huffle scraped the ground. He seemed cross that she had stopped dancing with him.

"Sorry," Grace smiled, dropping into a wobbly curtsy as if the dragon was a prince at a ball. Then the two of them stomped away together again, wiggling and turning in circles. Hetty was laughing so hard that she nearly fell off Billy.

"If only Huffle could be my partner at the Ballet of the Flowers," sighed Grace. "I don't suppose anyone would notice what I was doing with my feet if I had a real baby dragon dancing alongside me."

At last, when everyone was exhausted,

they unsaddled Billy and let the unicorns graze.

"Now we will have to get Huffle back into the cave," said Grace. "We can't leave him wandering around out here."

It took them over an hour of calling and cooing and coaxing, "Come on, Huffle. Come on." But the little dragon was having far too much fun; he and Chalky had started dashing around again.

At last, Grace managed to catch him with one of Billy's reins and lead him back through the cave.

"Push against his bottom, Hetty," said Grace, as she squeezed through the crack. "I'll pull from the front end."

The thin leather of the reins hardly seemed strong enough to haul the growing dragon's weight. "At least he can't fly yet," panted Hetty, falling in an exhausted heap on the ledge as they finally got Huffle back to his nest.

"No," agreed Grace. She felt sad for a moment. As soon as he could fly, Huffle would take to the skies and leave Coronet Island for good. Even in the old days, the crimson dragons had never stayed here all year round – it was only the females who returned, and then only to lay their eggs and nest.

Grace breathed in deeply and tried not to be unhappy. It would be good for Huffle to be free, to fly far away across the oceans exploring the world as soon as he was big enough to look after himself. It was her job to keep him safe until his wings were strong enough to take to the sky.

"We'd better find something to put across the crack," said Grace, heading back to search the glade. "We can't have Huffle wandering about the woods when we're not here. Someone might see him. Or he might find his way to school."

"How about that?" Hetty pointed to a heavy branch. The two girls dragged it through the cave and wedged it across the gap that led out to the ledge.

"Perfect,' said Grace. "That should keep him out of mischief for now."

"Uncle Falcon has a proper old dragon halter hanging in his shed," said Hetty. "It is made of copper thread, plaited a hundred times and twisted with a hundred turns. Nothing could break that. If we want to let Huffle out again tomorrow we can use that to lead him with."

"Great idea," said Grace. "Huffle is so strong, I was worried that Billy's reins were going to snap."

But when the two girls met at the edge

of the glade next morning, Hetty shook her head.

"The dragon halter has gone," she said. "It's been hanging on the same nail in the shed for years. Now it's completely disappeared."

CHAPTER TWENTY
The Outdoor Theatre

Grace and Hetty spent all day Sunday playing with Huffle in the glade again. Then they tucked him snugly in his nest. Without the dragon halter they had to use Billy's reins to lead Huffle through the cave once more. Then they blocked the gap in the wall with the heavy branch to keep him safely penned on the ledge.

All too soon the weekend was over, and it was time for Grace to face double Monday morning ballet class yet again.

"How time flies," said Madame Lightfeather, gliding into the studio like a swan in a white tutu. "We will be performing our Ballet of the Flowers in less than a week."

There was an excited gasp from the other twelve princesses and a single groan from Grace. Even shy Scarlet seemed excited by the chance to perform.

"You're going to be brilliant," whispered Grace, who had seen her friend's poppy ballet getting better and better as the weeks went by. Scarlet's feet barely seemed to touch the floor. She was like a floating red petal, spinning in a spring breeze.

"I could help you," whispered Scarlet, shyly. "If you didn't think I was being bossy, that is."

"Oh, yes!"

Madame Lightfeather was still talking to

the whole class. Grace had been so busy whispering with Scarlet that she only caught the last four words.

". . .in the Gemstone Glade," finished Madame Lightfeather, clapping her hands.

Grace felt the colour drain from her face. "What's she saying?" she hissed, grabbing Scarlet's hand. "Why's Madame talking about the Gemstone Glade?"

"Because that's where the show's going to be, stupid. Don't you know anything?" said Precious, butting in.

"We've all been talking about it for weeks," laughed the twins.

"Quiet back there," hushed Madame Lightfeather. "I want to see you all practising your steps."

How can I not have known? thought Grace. Then she realized she'd hardly spoken to anyone in her class since the ballet was announced. She was always busy with Hetty and Huffle.

"It was on the invitations," whispered Scarlet. "I thought you knew."

Grace had never seen the new invitations, but she remembered clearly picking up a muddy card on the day that she had ruined the old ones. Why hadn't she noticed then?

"Of course," Grace groaned. Billy had chewed a great chunk out of the card so that she couldn't read the time or the place of the show.

"I've never been to the Gemstone Glade," whispered Izumi. "But I thought I might go after school and paint. There are supposed to be blankets of flowers that look like jewels."

"You'd love it!" said Grace, without thinking. She clapped a hand over her mouth.

"Have you been there?" Izumi asked.

"Yes," said Grace. "No . . . I don't know."

Izumi looked confused. Grace turned and danced away as fast as she could. As soon as class was over, she'd have to find Hetty and warn her about what was going on. They must find a way to keep Huffle a secret or the whole school would be in a panic, even though he was still so young and no real danger to anyone. Keeper Falcon would be sure to drive him away from the island.

"After break, you are going to have fittings for your costumes instead of lessons," Madame Lightfeather said brightly. "Please organize a list amongst yourselves and then visit Fairy Godmother Pom in the Sewing Tower one by one."

"I'll go last," said Grace quickly. That might just give her enough time to find Hetty before anyone noticed she was gone.

The moment ballet class was over she

rushed towards the dovecote in the garden, pulling on her riding boots but not bothering to change out of her tutu.

There was no sign of Hetty. She wasn't with the doves or the peacocks.

Grace dashed desperately towards the stables, glancing at the big clock above the gate.

She wouldn't need to be back to see Fairy Godmother Pom for her costume fitting until five minutes before lunchtime. Surely measuring the yellow-brown dragon's heart smock that had been designed for her wouldn't take long.

"That will give us plenty of time to ride to the Gemstone Glade and see what's going on," Grace said to Billy. She jammed her riding hat on her head and grabbed a spare one in case she met Hetty along the way. She leaped on to Billy's back and turned him towards the gate. Her tutu stuck out all around her like a circus rider as she galloped away.

Grace was only halfway to the Glade when she saw Hetty dashing through the woods towards her.

"Quick," panted Hetty. "Have you heard? My uncle says he has to work in the Gemstone Glade to get it ready for the Ballet of the Flowers. That's where the show is going to be."

"I know," said Grace. "Jump on!"

She grabbed Hetty's arm and swung her up on to Billy's back.

"Hold tight," she said, putting the hat on the little girl's head. The two girls clung tightly to the unicorn as they galloped away.

Th.. Chalky appeared beside them from

"Hello, have you come to help us?" cheered Hetty.

"If only he could," said Grace.

Both girls fell silent as they skidded to a stop in the glade.

"Oh, no!" Grace gasped. "What do we do now?"

The flowery clearing was filled with a hundred shiny gold chairs all lined up in rows.

"They've blocked the entrance to the cave," said Hetty. "Look."

A huge wooden stage had been built against the rocks. A billowing red silk tent hung above it like a theatre curtain and a backdrop painted with garlands of spring flowers rose high into the ivy above.

"Poor Huffle," cried Grace. "He's trapped out on the ledge. He can't fly away, remember? He's still too young for his wings to work."

She thought desperately of the branch they had used to block the crack. He couldn't even come into the cave.

"It's good he's stuck out there," said Hetty wisely. "At least while the ballet is on."

Grace nodded. "I suppose you're right. But we still need to get to him. We need to feed him. We're the nearest thing to a mother that he has."

"The workmen must have gone for lunch," said Hetty. "Uncle Falcon came home to get a sandwich. That's how I found out he was helping to get ready for the show."

"Come on, then," said Grace. "We don't have long. We have to find a way to squeeze behind this wooden backdrop and check that Huffle is all right."

The girls ran to either side of the big stage.

"It's hopeless over here," cried Grace.

"They've pushed the boards snug against the rock."

"There's a tiny gap here," said Hetty. "Come and see."

Grace scrambled over the stage pushing the billowing red curtain aside as she jumped down the other side.

Hetty was pointing to a round hole at the bottom of the boards, not much bigger than a dinner plate. Squinting through it, they could just see the darkness of the cave beyond.

"Let me try to squeeze in," said Grace. But the gap didn't even reach her knees. "I'll never fit through in this thing." She wriggled out of her big, ruffled tutu and threw it to the ground.

"You'll never fit through even without it," laughed Hetty, as Grace tried hopelessly to wedge her shoulder into the narrow space. "But I can! I'm only half your size."

Without another word, she popped herself through the tiny gap and grinned back at Grace from the other side. "See?"

"Brilliant!" cheered Grace.

"I'll go to Huffle," said Hetty. "Don't worry. You head back to school. Bring milk in a small jug later so it will fit through the gap."

Grace could hear the sound of crunching stones as the little girl scuttled away into the cave. She thought how dark it must be with the entrance blocked.

"You're so brave, Hetty," she shouted.

"I'm fine," came a tiny call in reply. But then Grace heard the sound of voices coming through the woods. The workmen must be returning to finish work on the stage. She knew she had to go.

As she turned back to the glade, she realized she had forgotten to tie Billy up.

The shaggy unicorn was wandering among the rows of empty chairs with Chalky. They were pushing them over with their noses.

"You naughty boys," said Grace, but there was no time to put anything right. She grabbed her tutu and pulled it over her head like a ruffle. Then she vaulted on to Billy's back and galloped away from the glade.

Chalky refused to follow. He pawed the ground and whinnied desperately, looking longingly towards the stage at the place where his beloved Hetty had disappeared.

CHAPTER TWENTY-ONE
Dress Rehearsal

The following day, Grace stood in the Gemstone Glade with the rest of her class, ready to take part in the dress rehearsal.

She had made plans with Hetty; everything was arranged. Hetty had promised that as soon as she'd fed the peacocks that morning, she would come back to the cave and squeeze through the tiny gap under the stage.

She should be out on the ledge with Huffle by now, and she would stay there until the dress rehearsal was over. If there was any problem – any real problem – she would blow her horn and Grace would try to find a way to help. But both girls agreed that there wouldn't be a problem. There was no way that Huffle could get out into the glade, for a start. He was far too big to fit through the gap under the stage, and he couldn't fly up the cliff face either because his wings still didn't work. Hetty had three jugs of milk with her, so Huffle wouldn't go hungry. They'd do the same thing all over again tomorrow for the real show.

All Grace had to do was concentrate on her dance. This was her very last chance. She had to find something – *anything* – good enough to perform at The Ballet of the Flowers in front of a full audience. All she had so far was some stomping, some tramping and some wiggly-jiggly arm waving. It was going to be a disaster: a total disgrace.

"I'd much rather look after a baby dragon," she groaned under her breath.

Grace glanced around the glade. It was beautiful. The magical ring of jewel-bright flowers were at their springtime best. Every bud was open, glistening in the sun. And up on the stage, the other princesses in her class looked just as dazzling.

There was Scarlet, in chiffon as red as her name, and as vibrant as any poppy; Izumi in a delicate, water-lily-white tutu fringed with pale pink; even Precious looked magnificent in a gown of purple and black sequins, like her poison orchid.

Grace looked down at the shabby costume she'd been given.

"It's my own fault," she sighed. She'd been so busy running around the glade and making secret plans with Hetty that she hadn't had time to visit Fairy Godmother Pom for her fitting. The yellow-brown smock was much worse than she thought: it was far too short above her knees, but so wide that there was room for three of her inside it.

"Ha! Look at Princess Disgrace," sneered Precious, spinning past. "She looks like a long-legged ostrich in a sack."

For once Grace had to agree with her cousin.

"Come," said Madame Featherlight, raising her arms so that the scarf around her shoulders spread out like an emerald peacock tail. "Now that everyone is in their costumes, I want to see you all up on the stage together beginning to warm up."

"Right," Grace said to herself as they gathered under the beautiful red silk canopy. "This is it . . . no more disasters . . . no more distractions . . . no more dragons. . . All I am going to think about until tomorrow is this performance."

She bit her lip in concentration and rose up on to her toes. She wished it wasn't too late to find the perfect dance to please her wonderful, creative ballet teacher. She longed somehow to become that dragon's heart weed. Grace waved her arms in the air in a way she hoped might look like ragged petals in the wind, as Madame Lightfeather brushed past her.

"Lovely," grinned the teacher. Then Grace overbalanced.

"Whoa!"

She fell to the floor with a crash that was more like a falling tree trunk than a flower stem.

"Look out!" she cried as she bumped against Trinket, who bashed into Truffle, who banged into Precious, who collided with Christabel, Emmeline and Visalotta, who sent Latisha, Martine, Rosamond and Juliette tumbling like dominoes along the front of the stage until they landed in a heap on top of Scarlet and Izumi.

"Now look what you've done! You've knocked over the whole class," wailed Precious. "That's a record even for you, Grace."

"Clumsy idiot," squealed the twins.

"I really am sorry," said Grace, as Scarlet and Izumi poked their heads out from under Rosamond and Juliette's tutus.

"To your feet. Dance on!" cried Madame Featherlight, adding, "So long as no one is hurt."

Grace was relieved that some of the girls had even seen the funny side and were giggling as they clambered to their feet. Martine and Latisha were holding each other up, they were laughing so hard. But Precious silenced everyone.

"We won't be laughing if Grace does something like that tomorrow in the real show," she sneered.

Grace flushed with shame.

"Perhaps it would be safer if everyone found their own space, somewhere around the glade," said Madame. "Ignore all the other people around you. Find the dance within yourselves and try to bring that out. You have twenty minutes, then I'll see you all back here on stage."

The girls scattered in every direction, straightening their ruffled costumes and beginning to lose themselves in their own particular dance.

Grace hurried away, her cheeks still

burning with embarrassment. The other princesses must think her hopeless. She couldn't even look Scarlet in the eye, remembering how just yesterday her friend had been offering to help her. But Grace had been too busy with Huffle.

She slipped into the trees where no one could see her. It was dark, the ground was uneven and there wasn't much space. But at least it was private. There was no time to feel sorry for herself. All that mattered was making this dance work.

Grace squatted as low as she could, then sprang high in the air, hoping it made her seem like the tough little weed, growing up through sharp rocks and stony soil.

"Is that the best you can do?" said a voice behind her.

Grace spun around. It was Precious. She was holding up her black and purple sequined gown to stop it from trailing on the rough ground.

"Go away," sighed Grace. She didn't have time to put up with Precious's silly teasing or to get into a fight. "I just want to practise this dance. I've been stupid. I didn't work hard enough and now I am trying to make up for it. So *please*, Precious, leave me alone!"

"I've got a better idea," said Precious. "Why don't you just say you've twisted your ankle? You're so clumsy, everyone will believe you. That way you won't have to take part in the show at all . . . and you won't bring shame on our family! There'll be school governors coming to the performance tomorrow who are connected to some of the most important royal households in the world. I don't want anyone to know we're related if you're stomping around pretending to be a *weed*!"

Precious hurled herself forward, doing a spiteful impression of Grace trying to dance and waving her arms in the air.

"Stop it!" Grace jumped out of the way as Precious almost collided with her. "I really will break my ankle if you're not careful."

"Look at me! I'm a dancing weed!" laughed Precious, really enjoying herself now.

Grace took another step back.

"Whoa!" Suddenly, she felt the ground give way beneath her.

"Help!" she screamed. Grace felt herself toppling over . . . but she was skidding backwards down a slope at the same time. Earth and stones were sliding away beneath her thin ballet shoes. There were no more trees behind her: nothing to hold on to.

"Precious!" she cried, clutching desperately at the hem of her cousin's dress. "Help me! I'm slipping off the edge of the cliff."

CHAPTER TWENTY-TWO
Hetty Blows the Horn

Whoosh!

Grace felt herself slithering and sliding down the rock face.

Precious had fallen too.

"Save me!" she cried — her legs wrapped around Grace's waist as if they were riding a toboggan backwards down a hill.

Grace tried to lean back and slow down. It was hopeless. The rocks sloped away beneath them.

"I really didn't mean to push you off

the cliff!" cried Precious, sounding truly horrified.

"I know," yelped Grace. "I didn't mean to drag you with me."

Bam!

"Dig your heels in now!" Grace screamed and the two girls came to a stop. They were perched on a long, narrow ledge of rock no wider than a book shelf.

"Don't look down," panted Grace as she glimpsed the glistening sea beneath them.

But Precious was looking up at the cliff face above them. They could hear someone calling their names.

"Grace? Precious? Where are you?"

It was Scarlet and Izumi.

"We're down here," bellowed Precious. "Do something! Save us!"

"No," said Grace. "Don't call them! They won't know the top of the cliff is hidden in

the trees either. They'll come too near the edge themselves."

But it was too late.

"Help!"

There was a swirl of red and white, twisting together like a ribbon dance. A moment later Scarlet and Izumi were on the narrow rock beside them – all sitting in a row.

"We just wanted to know where you were!" gasped Scarlet, her face paler than Izumi's water-lily costume. "We saw Precious following you into the trees and. . ."

"Thank you," Grace squeezed her friend's hand as they all caught their breath. She didn't dare to lean out on the narrow ledge and reach over to Izumi who was on the other side of Scarlet. "Thank you both," she said. "I've been an idiot lately. I don't deserve for anyone to come and look for me . . . and certainly not for you to fall down a cliff for my sake."

"We're safe — for the moment at least — and no one was hurt," said Izumi kindly.

"Should we call for help?" asked Scarlet.

"I'm not sure," said Grace. "We don't want anyone else to slip. . ."

"If only you two had gone for help in the first place instead of falling down the stupid cliff yourselves," Precious sneered at Scarlet and Izumi

"None of us would be here if it wasn't for you," said Grace, "and I think you should remember that, Precious."

"Why? What happened?" asked Izumi.

"Nothing." Grace shook her head. She was fed up with arguments and fighting and people blaming each other for one thing and another. There had been quite enough of that this term already. It wasn't going to help anyone now. "Let's just say Precious had a new idea for my dance and it didn't quite work out the way that she planned."

A seagull flew by, looping-the-loop in mid-air and doubling back to fly past again as if he couldn't believe what he had seen.

"We must look like four china ornaments perched on a bookcase," laughed Izumi.

"As long as we don't fall and break," shuddered Scarlet.

"We need to do something," said Precious. "We can't just sit here for ever. HELP! HELP! HELP!"

She didn't seem to care that someone else might slip down the cliff, exactly as Scarlet and Izumi had. She just bellowed for all she was worth.

"The wind's blowing in the wrong direction, anyway," said Grace. "I don't think anyone will hear us." She tossed a blade of grass into the sky and watched as it blew away across the sea.

"HELP!" Precious screamed again.

Pom! Pom! A bright sound answered from somewhere just below.

"What was that?" asked Scarlet.

"It's Hetty!" said Grace. "She's blowing her dragon horn."

Of course! The ledge at the back of the cave must come out below here.

Grace leaned forward and glanced over to her left, daring to look down at last.

There was the tiny figure of Hetty, waving up at them from the ledge just a little way beneath them. Huffle was beside her in his nest, of course.

"There's something I need to tell you," said Grace, turning towards Scarlet and Izumi. "I should have told you sooner. Hetty and I found a. . ."

Pommmm! Pommmmmmmmmmmm! Hetty was blowing the horn for all she was worth.

"A dragon," gasped Izumi.

"Kill it!" screamed Precious.

"Don't be horrid. He's only very tiny," said Grace.

Scarlet was tugging at the sleeve of Grace's tunic, opening and closing her mouth as if trying to find the words to speak.

Grace saw a look of horror in her friend's eyes.

"That dragon is *not* tiny," gasped Scarlet.

Grace turned her head to see the dark shape of a great winged beast filling the sky.

It was the huge Coronet Crimson dragon she had seen all those weeks ago on the cliffs.

"Huffle's mother," croaked Grace. "She's come back."

The enormous she-dragon was thrashing her tail in the sky. Her sharp claws glinted in the sunlight as she swooped towards them from across the sea.

"She's even bigger than I remember," shivered Grace.

CHAPTER TWENTY-THREE
A Daring Leap

"HELP!" cried Precious, Scarlet and Izumi all together.

Please let someone hear us, thought Grace

Pommmmmmmm! Hetty was blowing her horn as if her life depended on it.

Suddenly, Grace realized exactly what was happening. Hetty's life *did* depend on scaring the enormous dragon away. Or – impossible as it seemed – on calming her down somehow.

The little girl was alone on the ledge

with Huffle. The mother must think she was trying to harm her baby.

"Run into the cave, Hetty!" screamed Grace, hoping her voice would carry down to the ledge below. "Squeeze through the crack and get away."

But almost as soon as she spoke, the dragon's huge tail thumped against the side of the cliff as she turned in wide circles, flying above her baby.

Rocks and boulders came tumbling down.

Hetty leaped out of the way, but even from up here Grace could see that her escape route to the cave was now blocked by rocks and rubble.

Pommmmmmmmmm! Pommmmmmmmmmmmmmm! Hetty still blew bravely – hopelessly – on the horn for all she was worth.

Grace had to think of a plan.

The dragon circled again, higher this time, never taking her fiery eyes off her baby or the little girl on the nesting ledge below.

Grace saw that the dragon was wearing some sort of bridle over her head – a halter of thickly-plaited copper rope. A broken length of rusty chain dangled from her neck.

"Someone captured her," gasped Grace. "That's why she abandoned Huffle in his nest. She couldn't get back to him. But now she must have snapped her chains and escaped."

"Help!" Hetty screamed, as the dragon swooped low to the nesting ledge once more. The sharp ridges of the creature's spiky back were level with the shelf where Grace and the other princesses were perched.

"Poor Hetty," screamed Scarlet.

"The dragon will kill her," said Izumi.

"Go on! Eat the servant girl, not us," hollered Precious.

Grace couldn't bear to look. But at the very last moment the dragon turned, quick as a fish in water, and flew back out to sea.

"Is she leaving?" asked Izumi. "Is she going away."

"No." Grace watched as the dragon flipped around again. "She's coming back more slowly, that's all. When you're as big as a dragon it's hard to land."

It looked almost like a ballet turn as the giant creature arched her back and pointed her long clawed toes.

"She has to land just right or she'll skid straight past the nest," said Scarlet, understanding exactly as a dancer would. Grace nodded. But she wasn't thinking like a dancer. She was thinking of something else: Billy.

She knew she had just one chance to save Hetty. She would have to act quickly as the dragon came in again to try and land.

"Lean back and hold tight to the rock," she said to the other princesses. "When the dragon drops below this shelf, I'm going to jump. I'm going to ride her."

"No!" gasped Scarlet.

But Grace was already tensing her knees.

"Hold tight to the rock," she said. "The dragon will be surprised when I fall on her back. She'll probably thrash her tail about and twist and turn. Don't let her knock you off the shelf."

The enormous beast was circling back, slow and steady this time.

"Are you sure about this?" asked Scarlet, squeezing Grace's hand.

"You'll never be able to do it," said Precious. "Never in a million years."

"Yes, you will," said Izumi.

"Grace can ride anything," agreed Scarlet.

And then the dragon was there. Grace knew she only had one go to get this right.

She saw a gap between two of the jagged spines on the creature's shimmering crimson neck.

"Here goes!" she cried.

Grace sprang forward.

Time seemed to stand still. She was falling. She felt as if she would never stop.

Then – THUD! She was on the dragon's back. She could feel the leathery skin against her bare knees under the tunic. It felt rough like tree bark, but also warm to the touch, as if a great coal fire was burning inside the dragon's belly. Grace grabbed the giant spike in front of her and clung on for dear life.

"Whoa!" Just as she had expected, the dragon twisted as soon as she felt Grace's weight land on her back. The creature turned, heading back out to sea again, roaring and spitting flames.

"All right, Old Mama. No one's going to hurt your baby," Grace soothed, patting the ancient fiery beast and leaning forward along her neck.

If she could just catch hold of the swinging length of chain, she could control the enormous dragon from her halter. Whoever had captured the Coronet Crimson had harnessed her mouth with a great iron bit.

The dragon twisted again. Her neck swung upwards. The chain bounced and jingled. . .

"Got it!" Grace felt a ring of cold metal in her hand. She pulled the chain back towards her like a pair of reins. "Steady, Old Mama. Steady now."

The dragon arched her neck, kicking her back legs wildly in the air.

She's trying to buck me off, thought Grace. But Billy had tried that once or twice. Grace just gripped harder with her knees.

"Steady," she soothed again. "I'm going to save my little friend Hetty, and then you can have baby Huffle all to yourself."

Grace turned the dragon's head towards the cliffs again.

"Are you mad?" cried Precious. "Take that monster away. Take her out to sea."

But Grace knew what she was doing and now she saw a chance to rescue the princesses as well as Hetty.

"Jump on!" she cried, pulling hard on the reins and shouting to Scarlet, Precious and Izumi. "You have to ride the dragon. It's the quickest way down from the cliffs." She was almost close enough to reach out and take Scarlet's hand.

"Trust me. If you're on the dragon's back, her flames can't reach you. Her claws can't scratch you," said Grace. "You have to believe me. It's the safest place to be." Scarlet looked terrified, but she was the first to jump. Izumi followed seconds later.

"Safe?" asked Grace, twisting her head to see her friends behind her on the dragon's back. There was plenty of room for them all – the huge red dragon was even bigger than a flying rhinoceros. More like two rhinos, really.

"Safe!" breathed the two princesses.

"Now you, Precious," urged Grace. Her arms were aching from pulling on the chain to hold the dragon steady.

"No way," screamed Precious. "I don't trust you. You have no idea what you're doing." She picked up a shower of stones and threw them at the dragon. "Shoo, horrible monster!"

Whoosh!

A blast of flames scorched the shelf. Precious jumped back and cowered against the cliff.

"Don't frighten her," cried Grace. "You'll only make her angry."

"Shoo! Ugly lizard!" Precious hurled more stones.

"Giddy up!" Grace kicked the dragon forward, urging her downwards. If Precious was stupid enough to torment the enormous creature, it was too dangerous to stay.

Now to rescue Hetty. This was going to be more difficult.

"Hold tight," she said, shouting back across her shoulder to Izumi and Scarlet. "I'm going to try and steer the dragon so that we fly close to the nest but she doesn't actually land. If she does that, she'll chase

Hetty into a corner. Remember, all she wants to do is protect her baby."

"Got it," said Izumi, loud and clear.

"Got it," whispered Scarlet.

"And kick your legs," said Grace. "Kick hard as if you were riding a unicorn. We want to keep this dragon moving while we snatch Hetty and pull her on board."

Grace thought of the gymkhana games they played on their unicorns: they had to lean down and a grab a flag from the ground without slowing to a trot. Grace was good at it. Riding lessons were the only time she ever got a merit at school. But grabbing a flag was a lot easier than snatching up a wriggling, frightened girl . . . and manoeuvring Billy was much simpler than trying to steer a furious, fiery dragon.

Grace loosened her grip on the chain a little and kicked her legs hard.

Whoosh! The dragon plunged downwards like a stone.

"Whoa! Steady up, now," cried Grace, pulling sharply on the chain as soon as they were level with the ledge.

The dragon fought and tossed her head.

"I'm not strong enough. I can't hold her!" cried Grace. But she felt Izumi's arms grab her around the waist. The two girls pulled back together. Then there was another tug. Scarlet must be pulling Izumi too. The three girls heaved, straining backwards in one long line, as if they were in the funny fairy tale about the giant turnip and were helping to pull it from the ground. Grace smiled to herself for just a second. Why did she never end up in the sort of fairy tales with glass slippers and moonlit dancing?

"Heave!" she bellowed. "Keep pulling." She felt the weight of the dragon's bit in its mouth. She was in control again at last. They were beside the nesting ledge. Hetty was running forward.

Grace knew she only had a second. Gripping the chain-like reins in one hand, she held the other out towards the terrified girl.

"Jump!" she cried. "I'll catch you."

CHAPTER TWENTY-FOUR
A Mother's Love

"Again! Again!" cried Hetty as she landed safely on the dragon's neck. She was sitting in Grace's lap. "That was the most fun I've ever had."

"Never again," laughed Grace.

"Never!" squeaked Scarlet. "I thought I was going to faint."

Grace loosened her grip on the dragon's chain as the giant creature landed beside the nest" We'll just have to be patient now," she said, patting the dragon. "We won't come to any harm up here on her back. She needs to see that Huffle is safe and well."

"He's adorable," cooed Scarlet, as the baby dragon bounded forward.

Grace explained how she and Hetty had found him.

"I'm so sorry I didn't tell you," she said.

"Don't worry," said Scarlet. "I'm just pleased I got to see him now."

"I agree," said Izumi. "Just look at that bright fiery crimson colour on his scales. It's like a sunset."

Grace smiled. Here she was, sitting on a real live dragon as it tended to its baby. She was cuddling Hetty, who was almost like a little sister to her, and sharing it all with the very best friends that anyone could ever hope for.

They all watched in silence, transfixed as the mother dragon nuzzled Huffle. She seemed to have totally forgotten that there were four girls perched on her back.

The only sounds were the little squeaks and whelps the dragons made, almost as if they were talking to each other, and the occasional cry from Precious carried down the wind.

"Get that thing back up here! I've changed my mind."

"Look!" said Hetty suddenly, leaning forward and staring between the dragon's pointy ears. "Have you seen her halter? It's copper rope. It's the one from Uncle Falcon's shed. I'd recognize it anywhere."

"Yes." Grace nodded. The first moment she saw it on the dragon's head she had been pretty sure it was the halter Hetty had described.

"But that doesn't make any sense," said Hetty. "Unless. . ."

Grace waited. She did not like the gamekeeper, with his narrow, angry eyes and his short temper. She did not trust him, either – the way he had been so quick to convince everyone that she was lying when Grace had said she'd seen the Coronet Crimson on the island. But he was Hetty's uncle, and the only family she had left. The little girl had to decide things for herself.

"Unless. . ." said Hetty slowly, "Unless it was Uncle Falcon who captured the dragon. It must have been him. Nobody else even knew that halter was in the shed."

Grace nodded.

"What I don't understand," said Scarlet, "is why he'd want to put a halter on her in the first place? He wouldn't need to tie her up if he was trying to drive her away from the island, would he?"

"He's a horrible, cruel man," said Hetty. "And he's greedy too. I bet he wanted to sell her to dragon smugglers."

"That's terrible!" cried Izumi.

"Thank goodness she was strong enough to escape," said Grace.

As if showing off her power, the enormous creature flapped her wings and shuddered underneath them.

"I think we're on the move," said Grace.

"Don't let her fly out to sea," gulped Scarlet. "I can't swim! I've never learned."

"Don't worry," said Grace. "The dragon knows now that we don't mean her baby any harm. I think she's taking us home."

Sure enough, the giant creature rose up into the sky and shot through the air like a rocket.

"Hold on tight," cried Grace with a rush of excitement.

Up the side of the cliff they flew, past Precious who screamed, "Bring that lizard back down here."

Above the Gemstone Glade they soared.

They saw their classmates spread out in all directions, searching for the girls who had disappeared from the rehearsal.

"Flying is amazing," whooped Hetty. "I never want to land."

The twins, who were right beside the stage, looked up and screamed.

"A monster! A monster!" they yelled as the dragon swooped towards their heads.

For a terrible moment Grace thought that perhaps she was wrong. Perhaps Coronet Crimson dragons *weren't* wise and gentle creatures who would only attack people if they were frightened or felt that their young were being threatened. Perhaps the mother dragon was going to dive down and gobble up Trinket and Truffle like two plump pork sausages.

But the huge creature flew steadily on.

Everyone in the glade was screaming now.

Then the dragon turned sharply and hovered low over the red silk canopy above the stage.

"Jump!" shouted Grace. "She's found us a soft landing."

The cradle of silk hung like a hammock below them.

Scarlet, Izumi and Hetty jumped.

Grace just had one more job to do.

She leaned forward as far as she could, stretching her body out along the dragon's neck. Then she pushed her fingers under the tight copper halter and slipped it forward over the dragon's ears. She watched as the harness fell to the ground, taking the heavy bit and cruel chain clattering down with it.

"Go on," she whispered, patting the dragon's neck. "Fly back to your baby. You're free now."

Then she leaped out into the air and waited for the billowing red silk to catch her.

CHAPTER TWENTY-FIVE
A New Home for Hetty

It was hours later, in the dark, after a long cold shower of spring rain, that Precious was finally rescued from the side of the cliff.

"I am never speaking to Grace ever again," she sobbed, shivering in her tattered sequin dress. "And as for that dreadful servant child, she should be sent away. And those dragons should be driven from the island too."

But Hetty was not sent anywhere. Nor were the dragons.

Lady DuLac would not allow it. The headmistress had listened to the whole story. And when guards were called from the mainland, Keeper Falcon confessed that he had captured the adult female the first day Grace had seen her. He had sold her to dragon fighters on a faraway island but he never dreamed that she would escape and fly back. He hadn't known that she had a baby to protect.

"Coronet Crimson dragons mean us no harm," said Grace. "They will only be a danger to us if we make them feel afraid or threaten the way they live."

"Princess Grace is quite right," said Lady DuLac. She turned towards Keeper Falcon, who was hanging his head. "You are a clever man who has studied the behaviour of dragons closely. Surely, if a first year princess has learned that we can live alongside these noble creatures, then you must have known that too. I think you have known it for years. Yet you wanted to frighten people so that nobody would ask too many questions when you removed the nesting dragons from this island."

"At least I got a good price for them," sneered the keeper.

"No harm shall come to the mother and baby now. They will be our guests on this island until the young one is ready to fly away," said Lady DuLac. "And, perhaps, if we are lucky, the mother will return to nest here again some day."

The guards stepped forward and put Keeper

Falcon in handcuffs – just as he had put the dragon in chains.

"What will happen to me now?" asked Hetty, standing on the steps of the Great Hall and looking out over the moonlit gardens as her uncle was led away to face a trial for cruelty to animals – not just to Huffle's mother, but also the dragons he had driven from the island and sold long ago. "Uncle Falcon never wanted me – but he is the only family I have left."

"You can stay here at the school if you would like to," said Lady DuLac. The headmistress crouched down and took Hetty's hands. "There are many fairy godmothers at Tall Towers who can look after you."

"Oodles of us!" said Fairy Godmother Pom, the cuddly seamstress, who was Grace's favourite teacher of all. She bustled forward and wrapped Hetty in her arms.

"You can have your very own room in the Sewing Tower," she grinned.

"But what about Flump?" asked Hetty, pointing to the big yellow dog. He was rolling on the lawn, which was still damp from the heavy shower of rain.

"He can come too," laughed Fairy Godmother Pom. "As long as he wipes his feet and doesn't get muddy paw prints on my material, mind you."

"He'll be good," promised Hetty, and all the princesses who had gathered around clapped and cheered, Grace loudest of all. Only Precious looked sulky.

"A servant girl!" she muttered under her breath.

"When Hetty is old enough, she can become a pupil at Tall Towers," said Lady DuLac, talking to the gathered crowd, but staring especially hard at Precious.

"She's not even a princess," gasped Precious.

"No," said Lady DuLac. "But she is part of our community. We will look after her."

"And she already has a unicorn. He has chosen her," laughed Grace. "Look."

Chalky was standing at the edge of the driveway.

When Hetty called his name, he came galloping across the lawn towards her.

"No unicorns in the garden!" cried Flintheart, who was standing amongst the crowd looking almost as sour as Precious.

"You will have to teach him not to do that," said Lady DuLac firmly, but with a little smile playing at the corner of her lips. "Off to bed now, everybody. We have a big day tomorrow."

"All the school governors will be here to see The Ballet of the Flowers," agreed Madame Featherlight from the top of the steps. "Dragons or no dragons, the show must go on."

By the time the girls came down to breakfast next morning, a stage had been built in the gardens.

"That's where the performance is going to take place now," said Princess Martine.

"We're not allowed anywhere near the Gemstone Glade anymore," said Princess Rosamond.

Big scrolls were hung on every notice board in the school:

Nesting Dragon
The gemstone glade is <u>strictly</u> out of bounds
All princesses are forbidden to go there until the nesting season is over.

REMEMBER: Coronet Crimson dragons will cause you no harm, but may attack if they are frightened or protecting their young. Keep your distance! Respect nature!

Even though Grace longed to see Huffle and his mother again, she knew this advice was right and that they should be left in peace.

"Dragons are wild animals, not pets," she said a little sadly to Scarlet and Izumi, as the three girls walked arm in arm across the courtyard.

"Sometimes it's difficult to tell the difference," laughed Scarlet, as Flump came bounding out of the Sewing Tower and nearly knocked them off their feet.

Hetty followed, looking sleepy and wearing a pair of snuggly unicorn pyjamas, which Fairy Godmother Pom must have found in the lost property cupboard and shortened to fit the little girl.

"She's going to make me unicorn curtains too," said Hetty with a big yawn.

"I bet she's already been sewing half the night," whispered Izumi. "You know how kind Old Pom always is."

"Oh, she has been up all night," Hetty yawned again, overhearing. "We both have. But we weren't making curtains. We were sewing on hundreds and hundreds of those little shiny things. . ."

"Sequins?" said Scarlet.

"That's right," nodded Hetty, as she wandered sleepily away to find some breakfast. "We had to make a new costume for Precious. She said hers was completely ruined on the cliffs."

"Typical Precious!" sighed Izumi. "She won't care a jot that the poor fairy godmother – and little Hetty – didn't get a wink of sleep."

Grace looked thoughtful.

She hadn't slept very well either. She'd been awake most of the night, tossing and turning and thinking about her dragon's heart dance. At last, just before dawn, it had all become clear in her mind.

"I know what I want to do for the Ballet of the Flowers," she explained to her friends.

"But I need to make a new costume too — a special one."

"That sounds exciting," said Scarlet.

"I was going to ask Fairy Godmother Pom to help me," said Grace. "But she must be exhausted after working on Precious's costume without a wink of sleep."

"Then we'll help you!" said Scarlet.

"Really?" asked Grace.

"I love sewing," said Izumi.

"I'm hopeless at it," laughed Grace. "I can't even thread a needle."

"True!" agreed Izumi. "But I'll teach you. After all, you taught us how to ride a dragon!"

"We'd love to help," said Scarlet. "That's what friends are for."

CHAPTER TWENTY-SIX
The Show Must Go On!

The Ballet of the Flowers was due to start in the evening.

The girls worked all day.

In the end it wasn't just Scarlet and Izumi's help that Grace needed, it was everyone's — even Hetty's. Only Precious refused to join in.

The First Year princesses bent over the long red silk cloth which had hung above the stage in the Gemstone Glade.

It had been brought back through the

woods and dumped at the foot of the Sewing Tower stairs.

"It's no good as a curtain for the show anymore," Flintheart had sighed. "The dragon's claws ripped it when she flew so low."

Flintheart scowled at Grace as she spoke, almost as if she thought it was her fault for not riding the dragon with more care.

"If nobody else needs the silk it will be perfect for my plan," grinned Grace. "It's the exact colour I'm looking for."

"I heard you wanted to make a costume from it," said Precious staring at the bright red silk. "That can't be right. Your flower is yellowy-brown . . . like mud."

"Yes. But you have to use your imagination when you're creating a dance," said Grace. "Isn't that right, Madame Lightfeather?"

"Of course," said the ballet teacher,

fluttering by in a fluffy boa of bright scarlet feathers which exactly matched the silk. "Take your imagination and *fly* with it, Young Majesty."

"I'll do my best," promised Grace. "With a little help from all my friends in the class. . ."

Fairy Godmother Pom helped too. When she woke from her nap, she made Hetty a shimmering waistcoat with sequins left over from Precious's frock. It was embroidered with crimson dragons, stitched with gold and silver thread on the tips of their wings.

"It's the most beautiful thing I have ever owned," beamed Hetty.

"You're going to look perfect. I *definitely* need you for my plan," grinned Grace.

It was a clear spring evening and the garden made a stunning setting for the Ballet of the Flowers. The grand school governors gathered on the rows of golden chairs. Many of them were emperors or kings and queens, their crowns flashing in the sinking sunlight, their white silk gloves shining like snowdrop petals against the green grass of the lawn.

Grace peeped round the edge of the thick velvet curtain that had been found to replace the silk one which had been ripped. She could feel flushes of fear leaping up the back of her neck like a dragon's flames.

Soon, every other princess had danced her piece. Izumi flowed like a river to represent a water lily, Precious was magnificent – and evil – as her poisonous plant, the twins were jolly as tulips and Visalotta shone like gold as a yellow crocus. The school governors clapped and smiled. They even gave Scarlet a standing ovation, rising to their feet and applauding for five whole minutes at the end of her beautiful poppy solo.

Scarlet blushed as red as the petals, but she was grinning from ear to ear.

Now it was only Grace who was left.

She strode out boldly on to the stage . . . and tripped over the edge of the thick curtain.

THUMP!

She staggered to her feet.

"I see Grace is still wearing that awful brown smock," sneered Precious, peeping out from behind the scenery.

"It's just for the announcement," said Izumi. "Shhh!"

Grace cleared her throat.

"My Lords, Ladies, Gentlemen and Most Royal Majesties," she began, curtsying with a wobble to Lady DuLac who was smiling encouragingly from the front row. "I know your programmes say that this evening's show will be a ballet, but I want to bring you something different . . . a dance which I have invited all my friends to join."

Pom! Pom! Pom!

Hetty, dressed in her sparkling waistcoat and a pair of flowing silk trousers, blew loudly on her dragon horn. At last, the bright, bouncy music perfectly suited the occasion.

A masked head of a dragon appeared between the velvet curtains. Izumi had hand-painted it and it looked beautiful: exactly like a magical, mythical, ancient, fire-breathing beast.

Grace smiled so that Scarlet, who was hidden inside the dragon's head, would know it was time to lead off with the rhythmic steps that all the other dancers would follow.

Now came the rest of the body as the first year princesses copied Scarlet's lead, snaking and twisting their way out on to the stage. Only their feet could be seen, in a long line, moving in unison like one mighty creature, below the billowing red silk costume they had all helped to make out of the curtain from the glade.

Only Precious stood alone, arms folded. She could be seen at the edge of the stage now that the thick velvet curtains had been flung back.

Pom! Pom! tooted Hetty. Grace held up her hand for a moment to make a last announcement over the music.

"My flower was called dragon's heart," she said. "I got stuck. I couldn't think of any way to make a dance . . . until I asked for the help of my friends."

Lady DuLac stood up and clapped. The audience joined her.

Grace turned and slipped behind her classmates into the very end of the long red costume.

"Here goes!" she chuckled and she thumped and stamped her feet to make the perfect heavy dragon's tail!

The royal crowd roared and cheered and stamped their own feet.

"Bravo!" they cried as the First Years performed a wild dragon dance on the stage.

Grace thumped the tail louder than ever. It felt so wonderful to be back amongst her friends again. To be part of Tall Towers life, where she knew she belonged and still had so much more to learn.

The dragon dance got three encores, which meant they had to do it all over again.

Madame Featherlight made a speech. "We have seen the hard work and imagination of a whole class come together here this evening," she fluttered.

Grace felt a warm glow of pride. With the help of her friends she had, at last, made a wonderful piece for the show. It wasn't a ballet – it wasn't very elegant either. But it was full of energy and joy – the perfect dance for spring.

It was only as the performance was finally over and the princesses lifted the costume to take a last bow that Grace looked up at the sky.

Flying in a silhouette against the sinking sun she saw the shape of two dragons, one big and one small.

"Look, Hetty," she cried. "It's Huffle. He's learned how to use his wings. He's flying. . ."

Hetty cheered and blew a wild celebration on her horn, *Pom! Pom! Pom!*

The crowd gasped. Some of the governors jumped to their feet in panic.

"Don't worry, the dragons will not hurt us," said Grace. "They are leaving the island now. This is only their nesting ground. They are flying off for new adventures."

Grace had expected to feel sad when she saw the dragons go. But instead she felt a rush of hope a sort of bubbling excitement that was a bit like the feeling she'd had when she first heard she was coming to Tall Towers.

The mother and her baby looked so beautiful – so free – against the fiery red and orange of the setting sun.

The crowd watched in silence until the dragons disappeared.

"Goodbye. Don't get into too much mischief, Huffle," Grace called. She rushed towards the front of the stage to wave one last time, forgetting that her feet were still wrapped up in the dragon costume.

Thud!

Every princesses in the class was pulled to the floor along with Grace. All except Precious, of course.

"What a disgrace," she said, turning to the audience.

But the royal crowd was laughing far too loudly to hear.

The First Years were giggling too, as they scrambled to their feet.

"We *all* look a total disgrace," they said, with tears of laughter streaming down their faces.

Grace beamed with joy as she untangled her feet from the costume.

"Let's have a round of applause for the dragons," she said, pointing up at the sky.

If you loved
Princess DisGrace
Second Term at Tall Towers
you'll love. . .

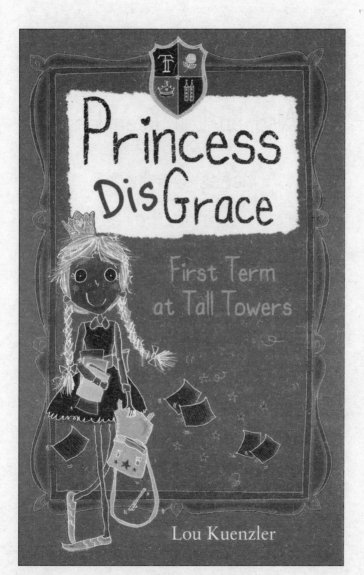

Princess DisGrace

First Term at Tall Towers

Lou Kuenzler

Also by Lou Kuenzler

LOU KUENZLER

SHRINKING VIOLET

DEFINITELY NEEDS A DOG

ACTUAL SIZE!

NORMAL size one minute, DOG BISCUIT-size the next!

LOU KUENZLER

SHRINKING VIOLET

ABSOLUTELY LOVES ANCIENT EGYPT

NORMAL size one minute, MINIATURE-size the next!